Two

Sebastian Beaumont was born in Scotland in 1960. He gained a degree in Visual Art and Creative Writing before moving to Brighton in 1987, where he lives with his partner, Simon. Beaumont's first two novel, *On the Edge* ('Mr Beaumont writes with assurance and perception . . .' **Tom Wakefield, Gay Times**) and *Heroes are Hard to Find* ('I cheered, felt proud and cried aloud – yes, real tears not stifled sobs – as the plot and people became real to me . . .' **All Points North**), are also published by Millivres Books.

Two

Learning to Drown
and
Addy, Laura and Old Jack Butler

Sebastian Beaumont

Millivres Books
Brighton

Published in 1994 by Millivres Books (Publishers)
33 Bristol Gardens, Brighton BN2 5JR, East Sussex, England

Copyright (C) Sebastian Beaumont 1994
The moral rights of the author have been asserted

A CIP catalogue record for this book is available from the British Library

ISBN 1 873741 17 0

Typeset by Hailsham Typesetting Services, 4-5 Wentworth House,
George Street, Hailsham, East Sussex BN27 1AD

Printed and bound by Biddles Ltd, Guildford, Surrey GU1 1DA

Distributed in the United Kingdom and Western Europe by
Turnaround Distribution Co-Op Ltd, 27 Horsell Road, London N5 1XL

Distributed in the United States of America by InBook, 140 Commerce
Street, East Haven, Connecticut 06512, USA

Distributed in Australia by Stilone Pty Ltd, PO Box 155, Broadway,
NSW 2007, Australia

Acknowledgements
To Simon Lovat, Keith Elliot, Tim Craven and Rob Cochrane for their
help with my manuscript.

for
Keith Elliot

Contents

LEARNING TO DROWN

ONE
BEN

The day my lover brought you back for lunch was the day my life began to change. He asked you because he'd seen that you were lonely, but I could tell that your motive for accepting his invitation was more complex than your need for company. You had predatory eyes and I realised, even then, that you would try to seduce him.

You had seen us together the previous evening dancing at Cruz, an unpredictable nightclub in the city centre, and mentioned this fact when you introduced yourself to him. I expect you mentioned how well Malcolm danced, or flattered him in some other flirtful way, and smiled your brutal smile and perhaps even touched him somewhere in a gesture of familiarity – on his elbow perhaps, or some other neutral place. I expect you mentioned that you had just moved to Manchester and knew no one – and Malcolm responded by inviting you back for a meal.

I felt a curious and contradictory sense of relief on meeting you, because I'd known that, sooner or later, someone would try to come between Malcolm and me. I was surprised to find that I had actually been waiting for this to happen, and was somewhat gratified to find that I'd been right to expect it. We had already courted change of this kind by experimenting, sexually, after we'd been assiduously monogamous for over two years. At the time I had found the experience simple and pleasurable. We'd gone to a nearby sauna and seduced a youth who was extremely good looking – by our standards – and we'd both enjoyed it. It was fun and it turned out not to be a problem at all, when I'd expected it to be devastating in one way or another.

But I can't bring myself to think about that day right now, because I can no longer see it as something unimportant. It seems, now, to be the pivotal point when future change became inevitable. I can't bring myself to examine what Malcolm's motives were in suggesting that

1

we go to the sauna, and nor can I bear to search for reasons to explain why I so readily agreed.

What makes that day so outwardly mysterious is that Malcolm and I loved each other. We were content in each other's company, but I lived in fear of change, not realising that change is the breath of life and I was strangling our relationship by trying to make it remain the same.

We were young. I couldn't bear to imagine that maybe I had not yet become fully adult. I'd thought that adulthood progressed immediately from adolescence, and that being adult meant never changing. The fact that I thought this proved, of course, that emotionally I was still a child.

When I saw you with Malcolm that day, I felt uncomfortable. Perhaps I was being unreasonably suspicious – after all, you are not the kind of man Malcolm usually goes for. I knew that even if you did fancy him, he wouldn't fancy you back. You are much more the sort that I find attractive – tall and bright and brash – and maybe that was another thing; I envied Malcolm the fact that you fancied him. Wires had been crossed. You should have been attracted to me.

Malcolm was jobless when he met you, in that post–graduation limbo of discovering that he had no idea what he wanted to do with his life. I was in the same situation, more or less, but I had enough freelance work using my computer to make it appear that I had purpose, when in fact I didn't. You were having six months off whilst you rearranged your life.

The major – and almost the only – fact of my existence with Malcolm to date had been our love for each other. Neither of us had had jobs after graduation and we'd spent that first summer idling away our time, waiting for the future to claim us. Then, I'd lost myself in the kind of literature that I would have been jeered at for studying, and I lost myself, too, in Malcolm's body, whose contours had never ceased to astonish me, despite their familiarity.

We had come to frequent the chic but somewhat posey café at the Cornerhouse, taking the bus from Chorlton once or twice a week, or walking in if we were broke, which was

2

often. Malcolm used to wander amongst the tables and converse indiscriminately with anyone who would talk. I, on the other hand, hid my shyness by becoming absorbed in my books, whilst secretly admiring and envying Malcolm's ability to be so fresh and vibrant and capable of finding interest in mundane conversation. But he always came back to talk to me, or to introduce me to the characters he had met. They were invariably strange, displaced people who had drifted here because they lacked direction – like ourselves. It was an unceasing pleasure to me, after watching Malcolm conduct an animated conversation with some exotic individual, to feel that he would return and sit beside me and stroke me somewhere – on my thigh or elbow or shoulder . . .

One reason for my happiness at that time was the fact that I'd previously thought myself lost. Before I met Malcolm I thought I had a terrible sickness from which I would never recover. The sickness was not my homosexuality, though in my time people have tried to convince me of this; it was my utter lovelessness. It was my burying myself in academia to escape from home and school and the pain of my childhood. It was the bleak landscape of futility that provided me with endless role–models for disaster.

My father had left my mother and she'd married a man who treated her as badly, if not worse. She'd always inflicted her unhappiness on me in a self–destructive way as if my love for her was an illumination within her misery so bright that she could not bear to face it. I continued to love her, confused by her lack of reciprocation, but it wasn't until I left home that I realised she hadn't shown her love for the simple reason that it was a precious commodity to be hoarded in secret; to be used as a weapon against her husband – my stepfather.

At first, Malcolm suited my belief that I was incapable of becoming close to people, emotionally. I'd been with him a year or more when we graduated, but we'd both been workaholic and life together had been something close to sexual expediency. So it came as a shock

3

for me to have unlimited time with him, because it was only then that I discovered that I was in love. This realisation came as a particular jolt because I had an entire future lined up for me back home near Sheffield. I'd been accepted as a graduate trainee on the local paper, the editor of which was Uncle Gordon – another deeply unhappy relative – and I had never imagined Malcolm as part of this future which loomed so large and uninviting and, until that moment, unavoidable.

And so I stayed on in Manchester and ignored the furious letters from my mother, and sat around in cafés with Malcolm and laughed about the absurdity of doing anything but loving him.

TWO
MALCOLM

Ben said he saw it coming, though it's annoying that he should say this after the event. He saw all sorts of disasters coming and the fact that one of them actually arrived doesn't make his prediction any more true in a general sense.

I saw Tag simply as a new acquaintance. I always felt a frisson when I met someone, and it wasn't a sexual thrill though I know Ben, in his blacker moods, thought that it was. It was sheer delight in human diversity, and the fact that no matter how uninteresting a person appears on the surface, there's always something fascinating underneath.

I didn't think Tag shallow or uninteresting when I met him at the check–out. I knew from the glint in his eyes that he was in need of friendship and had the desire to communicate. He had a resonant voice, with a touch of a Yorkshire accent. Ben says that when I brought him home for coffee he saw immediately that Tag had designs on me. But that was just Ben.

Tag did flatter me, I admit, though I didn't read any innuendo into what he said. He had seen me at Cruz the previous night with Ben and I knew that I was in no danger because he'd seen that I was hitched. When I brought Tag home, Ben was charming with him, and a little quiet, which was his way. He was even quiet with me sometimes which could be difficult.

We drank coffee together and Tag said that he'd grown up in Hebden Bridge in West Yorkshire, only a few miles down the road from Halifax, where I'd come from. Though I'd never met Tag himself, I do remember his widowed mother who ran a small newsagent in Mytholmroyd. She was a faceless nice person from my childhood, innocuous and maybe slightly dull. I may have shoplifted confectionery from her once or twice. I thought Tag was somehow familiar because of this, and appealing. I didn't see him as being available or desirable, though I can see

5

why Ben had his suspicions, seeing as there had been a certain precedent.

I think Ben blamed what happened between Tag and myself on the day Ben and I went to the sauna together – though I hardly dragged him there against his will. In fact, it was him that beckoned the guy into the cubicle. I, for all my extrovert ways, was incapable of making the first move. But Ben, once he'd got past the conceptual side of it, was keen and took the initiative, which shocked me.

It struck me, when he was grappling with the young man, that Ben had a great body. It was lean and taut, with a slim elegance that some had called thin, but which I recognised as angular and definite. Seeing him next to the boy, whose musculature was still shrouded by late adolescent flesh, I felt that Ben was disconcertingly beautiful. I sat there and it amazed me that I should ever have wanted more than Ben's extraordinary physical presence. I didn't have an orgasm when we had sex with this stranger – I just couldn't do it, especially whilst watching him and Ben getting so wild with each other. I just pretended I'd wanked myself off and left it at that.

The Youth In The Sauna, if he did anything, proved to me that Ben needed a damn good shake from time to time, because he was livelier after that and more sure of his love for me – or better at showing it, at least. I learned that meeting new people is the most important thing of all and that meeting them in the context of sucking their dicks is not necessarily the best way of going about it.

I think Ben was helped by the fact that The Youth appeared to fancy both of us equally. He'd always had this terrible insecurity that he wasn't as good looking as me, which annoyed me because his looks were one of my real pleasures and he always laughed it off when I complimented him. I think this insecurity must have been the result of his awful childhood, but wherever it came from, I found it irritating.

Although we have never discussed it, we both wondered if sex like this – casual sex together with a third party – would damage our relationship. But something had

6

to change because I knew that life was in danger of becoming monotonous. We were too self–obsessed; too cut off from others, despite my superficial social forays when we went down to the Cornerhouse. The exquisite summer of our graduation had passed, and a winter of foul winds and rain had come and we'd drifted into the anaesthesia of television on winter evenings. I would find myself feeling strange flares of panic at odd times as we sat and watched *Top of the Pops*, or yet another drama about people who *did* things with their lives. That's why I'd suggested the sauna.

I was wrong to suggest it, because sex was not the problem. I had a stupid, childish idea that sex and excitement are somehow interconnected; inseparable. But I loved Ben and sex with him was good. The problem was that we were poor. We'd spent most of our spare cash sitting around drinking tea, which was hardly constructive, but it got us out of the flat at least. We hadn't yet worked out how to have a social life without spending money. The result of this was that we saw less and less of our friends and watched more and more television in the evenings. And Ben didn't seem to mind. It was as though my company was, for him, endlessly sustaining.

Ben's biggest failing was that he was too easily satisfied with the present, he was too *certain* of things and didn't question them. He was too content with me. If only he'd seen me as being more fallible, perhaps he would have been happier about himself.

He was also suspicious. I know he didn't think of himself as a jealous person, and we never talked about this, but he hated it when other people fancied me. He hated it because he wouldn't see that people fancied him too, and he sometimes wallowed in a `what do you see in me' self–pity. I loved his modesty and insecurity and the fact that he didn't even know how good looking he was. I loved it and was infuriated by it at the same time.

That's why I used to go to see Tag without telling Ben about it first. I would go into town and then come back saying, `I dropped in on Tag on the way back', or `I bumped into Tag in town and we had coffee'. If I'd said,

`I'm just off to see Tag', Ben's face would have clouded over and when I came back he would be in one of his sighing moods. Maybe the fact that I could never be open about my friendship with Tag made me more clandestine and, in time, inevitably, more intimate. But this sounds as if I'm blaming Ben for what happened between us. It wasn't Ben's fault, but neither was it mine – or not in the cruel way that it must sometimes have appeared.

For the first weeks of our friendship, I didn't even think of the possibility of sleeping with Tag. Our conversations were all about travel and people and Manchester and so on, and besides, he wasn't really my type. But one day I came home and told Ben I'd seen Tag, and Ben made a comment – I don't remember what it was; something about the need to be careful – and the next time I saw Tag it was all different. I noticed the way he stretched his legs out with languid self–absorption. I noticed his unequivocal shoulders and I noticed that the way he looked at me was as uninterpretable as everything else about him. And I became intrigued.

We talked for some time about fitness and the fact that Tag went to the gym, then he talked a little about his childhood and then, briefly, about Ben. He asked me if Ben and I were faithful to each other, which made me blush because I was unwilling to answer yes, due to the sauna incident, and because I was enjoying this new feeling of flirtation. He read my fluster in one way or another and laughed and changed the subject, but he knew then that he could seduce me if he tried. We both knew.

Tag told me that Ben was weird, which came as something of a surprise to me because for so long I'd come to see him as intensely ordinary. But perhaps everyone seems ordinary once we're familiar with them. Ben had an ongoing momentum to his existence that encouraged me not to question the arrangement of our lives or whether it was in any way strange. Our days were always too easy for me to ever find them strange.

Of course Ben was weird. Wasn't that what fascinated me about him when we met? It just became invisible to me after a while because he camouflaged his weirdness with fragile domesticity. I now see that his cult of the ordinary stemmed from the fact that nothing about his life had ever been ordinary. As well as being rejected by his biological father, resented by his stepfather, and unable to communicate with his mother, there was his *terrible secret*.

As soon as I saw him I knew that he had a terrible secret. It was part of the myth that I was creating for myself at that time, concerning the sort of lover that I wanted. I wanted a man of mystery, a man who could be proud, aloof, alarmingly intellectual and yet tremblingly vulnerable at the same time. Ben was actually all these things and I fell in love with the concept of him long before I recognised him as a human being. And all the time I was trying to find out his terrible secret. I would drag him back to my room after lectures, or prolonged bouts of essay writing, and ravish him and get him drunk and try and prise out those precious nuggets of his past.

He relented eventually and told me of the summer's day he'd killed his younger brother in the garden. He'd just turned three, his brother was one–and–a–half, and they'd found some bandages whilst their mother had gone out on one of her `I'll be back in a minute' sorties that could drag into hours, and they'd played doctor. Ben wrapped his brother in bandages and pulled him into the paddling pool where he had drowned because he couldn't use his arms to right himself once he'd settled face down. Ben hadn't been aware that it was possible to drown in six inches of water.

He cried when he told me this, one of two occasions on which I saw him cry, but despite my fanatical interest in wheedling his secret from him, I found myself strangely disappointed by his story. I'd wanted *him* to be the victim, not the doer of the terrible deed. And I was shocked, too, because his story was so contrary to my understanding of life. I still had the idea – from reading too much Hesse and Gide – that tragedy is romantic. It isn't, or at least not for those who experience it, and I found myself feeling sympathy for his mother, whom I had set myself up to hate.

THREE
TAG

I'd had a shit–awful weekend. I'd been in London, which should have been a pleasure, but I discovered that a female acquaintance of mine had given Andy my new address and telephone number, the stupid cow. She thought that our fight was all my fault and that Andy deserved the right to be able to get in touch with me if he wanted. After a fight which ended with him throwing my camcorder into the toilet and smashing both the bowl and the recorder, I could have done without him knowing where I was.

Anyway, I was in Safeway buying some stuff – junk mostly – and I saw this cute number, so I followed him round for a bit, trying to get eye contact, but he was in a world of his own and didn't notice. I'd seen him the night before down at Cruz dancing with a fey looking guy; one of those slim types who look intellectual and mannered, with this long fringe that he was constantly fondling or wafting out of his eyes with a flick of his neck. But this guy in front of me in Safeway was dark and taut, almost a skinhead, and he looked like he could put up a bit of resistance if he wanted to. I'd tried to cruise him for a while the previous evening, but realised that he was an item with the skinny guy, which seemed a waste.

And here he was in front of me at the check–out. I watched him as he piled cheese and fruit onto the conveyor belt. He was unshaven and brusque in his movements and just standing behind him gave me a hard–on. I leaned round him to pick up the *next customer* sign and said, `Hi, didn't I see you last night at Cruz?'

He looked round at me and smiled in a kind of dark, spontaneous way and said, `Well, I was there so maybe you did.' I smiled back, my hardest, most carnivorous smile and said, `You dance very well. I couldn't help watching,' and he blushed. I knew I was in with a chance when he waited for me to pay for my stuff. We left the store together and he asked me where I lived, so I told him

10

and asked him if he wanted to come back for coffee. `I can't,' he said, `I've got some food on at home. Why don't you stop off for lunch?'

I thought I was really in, but when we got back to Malcolm's place, this other guy was there, Ben, the wimpy one. He slunk around in the background whilst I talked to Malcolm, and only came and sat down at the table when Malcolm served the soup. Ben was one of those incredibly *gay* looking people. He wasn't what you could call camp, but there was something soft about the way he moved that screamed *faggot,* and which I hate. He didn't participate in the conversation much, which didn't bother me. Malcolm was talkative and I told him a bit about my travelling, and he was impressed and I wondered what the fuck he was doing shacked up with someone like Ben.

When I left, I slipped Malcolm my address and number and told him to give me a ring. I gave him my `come on your own' look which he read perfectly and which made him blush again, so I knew I was going to have him sooner or later.

I walked home, picked up my kit, and headed for the gym. It was the beginning of my second month living in Manchester and I felt I'd arrived at last. I had a hard–on on and off whilst I pushed weights, especially the bench press and the concentration curls. I noticed one or two guys noticing it, but they were straight so I ignored them. When I got home I tossed myself off and wondered when Malcolm was going to call.

That night I couldn't sleep. I was on edge and bored, and ended up at around one a.m. taking a taxi into the city centre and cruising down by the Chester Street car park. I found some guy in the dark, next to one of the late–night cottages. He was wearing an anorak and a thick scarf but was still freezing. He'd probably been there for hours. He could hardly see me, but once I took him into the cubicle he felt my pecs through my sweatshirt and moaned, so I pulled his trousers down and fucked him right there, which was kind of seedy in a porny way. He was too yielding for me to really get into it. He submitted even

11

when I pushed his arse forward to get him in the right position. Being crushed against the cistern must have been uncomfortable, but he took it like a frightened lamb. I jammed my dick into his guts as fast and hard as possible – not because it made him squirm with pain or because he was enjoying it, but because I didn't want to lose my erection. When I came, I pulled away without looking at him and took a taxi home for a shower, and decided I'd have to be pretty desperate before I tried that again.

FOUR

BEN

I was born in Glasgow, although I left when I was a child, so I have hardly any recollection of the city apart from the art gallery and Charles Rennie Mackintosh, and the glasshouses of the botanical gardens.

My brother died when I was three. He was a year–and–a–half old, and the death seemed to send my mother a little mad. She would cling to me sometimes, and yet reject me at others so I grew up confused about the source and purpose of human affection. We moved away shortly after my brother's death, to Chesterfield, where we lived in sight of the church's crooked spire. My father had very little to do with me and treated me as though I was not his responsibility.

My father left my mother when I was nine. She had had a series of lovers throughout my childhood and I was used to strange men visiting her whilst my father was at work. After he left, my mother married one of these strange men and settled down to another life of unhappiness almost indistinguishable from the first.

I once ran into the bedroom when my mother was in bed with a man. He clouted me across the head, knocking me to the ground, and told me to piss off. I had no idea what they were doing, but it seemed to hurt them, and I learned to leave my mother alone when she went to her room to indulge in her strange rituals.

When I was sixteen I realised I was gay. I did not tell my mother and stepfather. I kept it to myself and wondered if I would ever meet another person who felt as I did.

When I was seventeen, I read a long article in one of the radical magazines about gay lifestyles. It was a revelation. It mentioned that there was a large gay community in Manchester, and so I decided to go and live there. I was studying English, Geography and History for `A' level at the time, and I applied to Manchester University to study English Literature. When I was there, I had a couple of brief affairs and half fell in love with an older man. Then I met Malcolm. We became lovers and, after graduation, we stayed on in Manchester.

I was unsure how to tell Malcolm that you had started looming on the horizon of my insecurities. What made it more difficult was the fact that, even after a couple of weeks of seeing you almost every day, Malcolm wasn't aware that the relationship between the two of you had become more than mere friendship. I don't know if I would go so far as to call it love, or lust or infatuation, but it was certainly more than friendship. What made me realise this, apart from the easy way you related to each other, was the fact that you were both slightly sheepish when I was around, as though in my presence you were unable to talk about the kind of things you would normally discuss. I accepted this because I think that it's valid to have secretive friendships, and it's good to be able to talk with candour about one's lover to a third party. But I was concerned about motives. Not of Malcolm's, but of yours, because you flattered him too much and there was always an understated innuendo to what you said that seemed to embrace him with your intimacy whilst excluding me. It made me irritable and perhaps a little jealous, though I couldn't be sure of that and accept that it's difficult to be objective about what one feels in circumstances like these.

I think I said something like, `Be careful, Malcolm. Tag is only trying to use you.' And Malcolm said, `Why do you think that?' So I tried to explain, but I failed because I wanted to sound objective, which I wasn't, and I wanted to talk of my suspicions without sounding petty, which I couldn't. And as I talked I could see the recognition in Malcolm's face. He hadn't seen it before, but now he realised that I was right – although he denied it – that you were deliberately making a play for him. And I could see that he liked the thought of it, that he was flattered and pleased by it. So, in a sense, I feel that I caused the whole thing myself. Maybe if I hadn't mentioned it in that way, Malcolm would have blindly gone on being oblivious – not that there's any point raking through the past to try and work out what might have happened under other circumstances.

A problem I had in my relationship with Malcolm was

14

that I always feared being too clingy with him. I know I had a tendency to grab hold of things that gave me security. I tried to keep hold of them to the exclusion of all else. It was because of my unhappy past, I know, but this knowledge didn't make it any easier to accept what I was doing, or facilitate an ability in me to change. I was clingy. Why I was clingy is perhaps irrelevant. The fact is that the result of my fear of clinging – and my fear of its destructiveness – was my decision to let Malcolm conduct his relationship with you without being heavy or judgemental.

I decided to trust him.

What surprised me after making this decision was that I became much more friendly towards you and felt less threatened by you. I kept imagining the sexual scenario that was by now, I felt, inevitable, and in imagining it I somehow became sexually involved myself. Visualising you having sex with Malcolm made me realise how much I was attracted to you. In my fantasy, the three of us became involved in an obscure but potent haze of eroticism that, although non–specific in a physical sense, was nevertheless obsessive, complicated and obscurely empowering. It made me feel that I was being deliciously perverted. Whereas in the sauna there had been a clear parameter of consent, in my imagination you and Malcolm lost any power of sanction over what I decided to make you do. And of course, with all these fantasies, my sex life with Malcolm took on a new frenetic dimension that was tinged by the shadow of change.

I don't know how Malcolm interpreted my increased fixation with his body, but he didn't question it and didn't seem to realise that our closeness was caused by the threat I felt in his relationship with you. I began to observe him more closely, to appreciate him more, which was a good thing, though I constantly worried about the ethics of how I was feeling.

Malcolm had thick dark hair that would have been curly if he'd ever let it grow long enough. It was buzz–cut from the nape of his neck to above his ears and it accentuated

15

the beautiful curve of his head. His sideburns – extending to the level of his mouth and shaved to a point – were so short as to be stubble, almost. He trimmed them every three or four days with a number one trimmer. He looked cute and dangerous at the same time, with eyes that appeared jet black from a distance, and straight, lush eyebrows that moved as he spoke. He had a small curl at the front of his hair that he would gel up into a Tin Tin tuft which I thought mind–numbingly horny. His ears were quizzically turned outwards so that he looked as though he was always straining to hear something. I loved his ears and enjoyed nibbling his small lobes and sticking my tongue down his ear hole until it made squishing noises with the saliva. He had a squarish chin and sturdy cheek-bones so that he looked as though he had extra–accentuated chiselled features. I could look at him for ten seconds and get an erection. And that was just his face. I could imagine his face, his wide lips, kissing your lips and I would find my breath becoming stilled for a few moments at the thought, and then coming out in a rasp.

And then, quite suddenly, I found the idea of him having sex with you a complete turn–off. It was like a switch being pulled. I realised that I hadn't thought sex between you was inevitable at all. I'd flirted with the idea of inevitability and allowed myself to be titillated by it. When I noticed you being more tactile with Malcolm and when, eventually, he said casually one evening, `Tag's popped the question', I realised that I'd never had a sense of reality about the situation at all. I found your question hugely threatening. Malcolm wouldn't say how you'd actually asked him, but I imagine it was something characteristically upfront.

I've come to the conclusion that questions of this kind aren't popped at all, they are skirted round, approached slowly, tested gently for signs of possible rejection and only then are they posed – when the answer is expected to be yes.

I now realised that my decision to trust Malcolm was an impossibility. There was too much at stake; principally, the only stability I'd ever experienced in my life. And, anyway,

16

trust is something that you don't make idle decisions about. It is either there or it isn't – you can't create it out of nothing. Then, of course, there's the conundrum: *If I say yes, I'll lose him. If I say no, I'll push him away*. In the end there was no decision to make. The only thing I could do was trust Malcolm, though as that seemed, at least for the present, impossible, I resolved to pretend to trust him instead. And to hope that I wasn't precipitating some calamity for which I could only blame myself.

It seemed so cool and casual and adult to say, `If you want to', when he asked my permission to have sex with you. Malcolm's request seemed at once the most honest and the most selfish question that could be asked. It was the most complete passing of the buck that I could think of. Maybe he realised this because he laughed when I answered him and he cuddled me and said, `I won't go, it's stupid. I love *you*. I don't really want to sleep with Tag, it was just curiosity.' But I knew he wanted to sleep with you; I knew that he would do it eventually whether I gave him permission or not. So I said, `Look, if you want to do it, do it, okay?'

And he said, `When?'

`As soon as possible,' I told him. `If this terrible itch has got to be scratched, then get it over and done with,' and with that he smiled, kissed me, then phoned you and arranged to go over straight away.

`Don't worry, Ben,' he said, `I love you,' and, leaving me to watch Eastenders, he walked across Manchester to spend the evening in your arms.

It felt weird, sitting there thinking about both of you together. The weirdest thing of all was that I didn't particularly mind; or at least not with the painful distraction that comes with bitter regret. I was pleased for Malcolm in a way. He was getting up and doing something that I had been idly tempted to do once or twice in the past, but which I would never have had the nerve to follow through. I was interested and frightened and realised, even then, that part of me wished that I had gone in his place.

So much of my life has been wasted wondering about

17

things and not doing them, that I'm impressed and envious that Malcolm wondered and then *did* it. But in the past it always seemed that I'd endangered everything by making any emotional movement. You go for something and then when you get back everything has changed. Everything has changed infinitely for the worse and you find that you didn't even get what you went for. When things have always fallen apart around you, what is there to make you believe in stability? Until Malcolm came I was lost to pessimism, and even when he gave me grounds for hope, it was still hard to change the habits of a lifetime.

But I knew I wouldn't be able to hold Malcolm with me in our limbo forever. I knew that, so it wasn't a surprise when he wanted more stimulation. I wanted more stimulation too, but he was so far ahead of me on that score that he'd discovered how to let go where I was still grasping at him and wishing I wasn't clutching, but clutching all the same. The sauna was one thing, but it had been a one–off event that I hadn't suggested and had never thought to repeat.

I wanted to think that you would do us both good, that Malcolm would come back and still be in love with me and I would see that I don't have to be obsessive or possessive in order to keep someone. I felt that perhaps I had caged Malcolm and the only way that I could really hold on to him was to open the cage and let him stay there of his own free will – that perhaps, by opening the door of the cage, the cage would cease to be a cage at all, and become a meadow or a beach or some other place of freedom.

And of course he did love me when he came back. He returned pleased and obviously relieved, and happy to see me, so I couldn't regret my decision to allow him to go. And anyway, we're all individuals. I think there's something a little sick about asking and giving permission, as though we own each other. I can't bear that, actually.

FIVE
MALCOLM

I was born and raised in Halifax. My mother took me to Manchester when I was seven and I was particularly impressed by the old, ornate buildings in the city centre – especially the Town Hall, which was incredible. Once, I visited an aunt who lived in an area of the city called Chorlton. I immediately felt at home and decided that one day I would live there.

My parents are happy together and showered both my sister and myself with affection. I told them I was gay when I was seventeen and they threw a coming out party for me. I hadn't realised, but they had several gay friends, whom they made sure I met and who were helpful, supportive, friendly and not at all pushy or intent on seducing me.

I had my first boyfriend when I was sixteen. It was an unhappy affair because he was a real closet case. I took my second boyfriend home to meet my parents and they gave us a talk about condoms, which was sweet of them, but unnecessary and rather embarrassing.

I met Ben at university and was fascinated by him immediately. He seemed so scarred by life, whereas I had arrived at the same age unscathed. I fell in love with him, despite his almost crippling shyness, and took him home to my parents where he blossomed incredibly in their acceptance. He didn't take me to see his parents. He informed them of his homosexuality by letter which solicited a hysterical meeting with his mother to which I was not invited.

I had such an idyllic childhood that it wasn't until I met Ben that I realised people could even HAVE an unhappy past.

✳ ✳ ✳ ✳ ✳

I walked over to Tag's place. It was a ground floor flat near the park, with an oblique view of trees and grass which made it seem peaceful. He was renting the place and had only moved in a few weeks before, so there was something dishevelled and student–like about it. We kissed

19

immediately and I noticed, from close up, that there were lines fanning from the corners of his eyes and a certain crumpledness about the skin immediately below his earlobes. I had never thought to ask his age, but had assumed him to be in his mid– to late–twenties. Now I realised he must be in his thirties and I found the thought a mild turn-off. I was twenty-two (Ben was six months younger than me. The Youth In The Sauna had been no more than nineteen). The strange thing about realising this ten year age gap was that it made me feel powerless. All my life I had been in situations where older people told me what to do – at home, at school, at university. Now, suddenly, I felt that Tag was in control.

`Are you alright?' he whispered, and I said, `Yes, why do you ask?' and he said, `No reason,' and took my arm and steered me through to the bedroom where we sat on the bed and kissed.

When we stopped to take our clothes off, I was disappointed by Tag's body, which was pale and a little too broad for me. I realised that I had had a specific idea of what his body would look like – sleek and lean, perhaps a little hairy. But it was sturdy, smooth, almost lumbering, and although he wasn't at all fat, his muscles were heavy; pumped up from regular visits to the gym. His stomach was absolutely solid, his abdominal muscles clearly delineated, and he looked, I thought, to be verging on the sporty middle-aged.

He had a scar across his chest which I asked about and he laughed, making it flex by tensing his muscles. `I used to tell people it was from a shark attack, but it's from a sailing accident I had when I was on holiday as a kid up near Whitby. A cable snapped whilst I was leaning against it and it sliced me open from here to here.'

I traced the scar with my finger and then with my tongue. Tag pushed me back on the bed, spread-eagled my arms and held me so that I could hardly move. Then he leaned down and licked my eyelids. I had never been in a submissive position before and although I wasn't sure I liked it, I found it arousing all the same. He smiled and lay on top of me, pushing the breath out of me, then he kissed me hard. I felt myself gag, which made him laugh and pull away.

He placed one hand, flat, fingers spread, on each side of my rib cage and pressed in, squeezing me. I reciprocated and we ended up in a sort of impromptu wrestling hold in which I was half on top of him. He tensed his arms and, with a peculiar flip, he twisted me over onto my back and lay on top of me again, panting into my face and smiling. Then he straddled me, knees on either side of my shoulders, and took my head in his hands. He pulled me forward and forced his erection into my mouth. I had wanted to do this of my own accord and was somewhat bemused by the way Tag seemed to have no concept of my consent. Ben and I had never wrestled or forced each other to do anything.

He leaned down and picked up a tube of K–Y and, squeezing a generous quantity onto his palm, he lubricated his circumcised dick, then tossed himself off for a while as I watched. At first he seemed oblivious of my presence, then he picked up the tube again and applied some more gel to his finger tips, which he smeared onto my arse in a movement so quick that I didn't have time to protest. I pulled away afterwards, but he hugged himself against me and twisted me round so that my face was pressed into the pillow and his dick was against my buttock. In a moment of panic I twisted back and pushed his dick away with my hand, gasping, `No', at him and feeling that, in just a few moments, I'd lost control over what was happening. I glared at him and, using all my strength, pushed him off me. It's incredible that you can spend all that time with a person and then they will do something so dangerous and unexpected, something so outside the bounds of permission, that it freezes you inside. I hadn't even considered mentioning the whole safe sex business – had taken it for granted. But Tag continued to smile, grunted, and just shook his head gently and took my hand and placed it on his dick so I could toss him off instead. I let my hand rest there, immobile.

`Why did you do that?' I asked him.

21

He snorted and cuffed me across the top of my head.
`It was a joke,' he replied. `I wouldn't have fucked you.'
`Even if I hadn't stopped you?'
`But you did stop me, didn't you?'

Tag straddled me again and looked down. He tousled my hair then leant down to kiss me, aware of my panic and allowing himself to be gentle for the first time. The image of him above me like that, muscles strained, was overpowering, disturbingly erotic, and this time I found myself disliking the powerlessness that he was obviously trying to invoke in me. He put my hand on his dick again, and with a feeling of, `Oh, well . . . ' I began to toss him off. He grabbed my shoulders and clung, leaning away from me, eyes closed, until he came, spattering my chest and neck. He paused, gasped for breath, then rolled away, lying beside me on the bed. After a few moments, he rolled back, took my dick in his hand and deftly began to wank me at great speed, without any body contact other than his hand. I closed my eyes and thought, not of Tag, but of how sexual energy can be so divorced from pleasure that orgasm becomes a detached physiological fact.

After Tag had finished, I lay on the bed, breathless, looking down at the debris on my stomach, bewildered by the contrast between my expectations and the fact of their consummation – bewildered too by the fact that, in spite of my ejaculation, I had felt almost nothing.

`That was great,' said Tag as he passed me a towel. `When can we do it again?'

SIX

TAG

I'd waited long enough for Malcolm to come round, but
I'm nothing if not patient. He had a kind of
open–yet–mischievous quality to him that always turns me
on, and he was bright and jokey and tactile. I knew he
fancied me, but he was also in love with Ben, which
annoyed me because anyone could see that Ben was
holding him back – keeping him from fully expressing
himself, both emotionally and physically. Malcolm had a
horny quality of subdued aggression, and I decided
definitely to teach him to express it. The problem with
Malcolm was that he'd never experienced anything in life.
He had a kind of blankness in him which needed to be
sorted out. He was not conscious of this, but it showed in
the way he grabbed at our friendship when we met, and
also in the kind of mild dissatisfaction he showed with life
in general – and that wasn't just because he was jobless.
His story about going to the sauna with Ben proved that he
had a real curiosity about life, and I could see that Ben was
stifling it.

The problem with Ben was that he had experienced too
much in life – too much of the wrong kind of things. When
I heard a bit about his past, I realised that was part of the
reason why he viewed life as though it was about to kick
him in the teeth. He had the look of a man who has thrown
a grenade and is cowering from the inevitable blast. But his
childhood only explained part of it. There was something
else that he either hadn't told Malcolm, or that Malcolm
wasn't prepared to tell me. I could have worked it out, I
suppose, but I wasn't that interested. Ben was in the way,
that's all. Why he was in the way wasn't of interest to me,
and I didn't want to delve into the sticky mess of his past.

In the meantime, whilst I got to know Malcolm better
and worked on his natural narcissism, we held bland

conversations about work, life and the future. I didn't care a sod what Malcolm wanted to do in the future; I just wanted to get him into bed and then take it from there. I listened, though, and kind of enjoyed the quiet preliminaries to fucking. When foreplay lasts weeks, or even months, it drives me demented but keeps me alive. I fed him lots of subversive anti–Ben invective, in a subtle kind of way, without actually making it appear that I disliked Ben or wanted to get in the way of their relationship.

When Malcolm came round one afternoon and we hugged on the doorstep as he came in, I noticed that he didn't pull away as fast as usual. Later, when I made him coffee, I put my arms round his waist and he put his hands on mine in a friendly but erotic way and I knew that the time had come, so I pulled him round and kissed him on the lips and felt his nipples through his shirt and rubbed his arse and told him we ought to go to bed. But he was freaked–out by the suggestion and said he'd have to ask Ben. Ask Ben! I knew he was young, but this was pathetic. Ben was no one, he wasn't even there, and it didn't matter a blind fuck what Ben thought. Still, I could see that Malcolm was on the verge of saying no forever, so I relented and let him go back to ask Ben if he could sleep with me sometime, and I pretended that I thought it was the wisest thing to do. When he left I tossed myself off and thought of Andy in London and thought of ramming his head down the broken bog and smashing his teeth out on the shit–stained camcorder and I thought, *Justice will happen, I'll get him back.*

It surprised me when Malcolm phoned up that same evening and asked if he could come round for sex. I told him to come over straight away and then went to have a shower. When he turned up, I kissed him immediately and let my hands wander up under his shirt. He seemed to only want to kiss at first, and it made me think he was maybe one of those kiss–and–cuddle types – which figured, seeing as he was going out with Ben – but then I thought that, no, it was because he didn't know what he wanted. I wondered how many lovers he'd had. Three?

Two? Only one? I guessed it was up to me to show him how much more there was to do than kissing . . .

On the bed, Malcolm just lay there like that pansy I fucked in the cottage, so I grappled with him and tickled him until he reacted – which he did eventually, wrestling with me and putting some real vigour into it. He had promising muscles that would have responded well to a bit of weight training, and I crushed them in my grip. After that, I noticed he was holding his arse in an appealing way, so I wondered if he wanted me to fuck him. I was going to ask him about it, but then I thought, *Just do it*. I lubricated myself and hoicked him onto his face, and gelled his arse, and he went kind of taut and hysterical, for a moment – like a rabbit in headlights – and then he went from being rigid to flailing around with panic. He twisted from under me, and pushed my dick away, gasping, `No, no', and I laughed and squeezed him for a moment in my arms, but he pushed me off so hard that I knew he'd bruised my lats, and I thought, *He's got it*!

Then he asked me why I'd tried to fuck him, so I told him it was just a joke. He was so obviously worried about Aids that I realised this was something I could use in the future – his fear. I don't have Aids, or at least I reckon it's unlikely given what I like to do in bed, but I'm not going to tell him that. Let him sweat. Let him fight me off. Let that thrill of fear be parallel to his lust and then sex with Ben will seem like flower arranging by comparison.

When Malcolm had calmed down, I got him to toss me off. It was clear that I'd gone as far as I could go – perhaps even a little too far – so I backed off and lay back and let him get on with it. I could see that on the surface he was upset, but underneath he was already hooked on me – on the power that I could bring to having sex. I decided to go easy the next time we went to bed, and then, gradually, I'd be able to squeeze the pleasure out of him.

SEVEN

BEN

Malcolm and I only fought once, right at the beginning of
our relationship – about sex and jealousy. That's why I
knew that sex with others could so easily change
everything. We fought about Richard, an older friend of
mine who was, to an extent, in love with me, but with
whom I had never slept.

Richard was a part-time lecturer in the English Depart-
ment. I hadn't been one of his students, but I'd met him at
a faculty social evening. We both came from the same part
of Derbyshire, which seemed reason enough for him to
invite me over for dinner with one or two of the other first
year students. That first evening I'd realised that he was
interested in me, though I hadn't yet realised that this
interest might be sexual. I liked him too, and readily
accepted a second invitation – to go over on my own.

He made a mild pass at me that evening, but I was only
nineteen at the time and someone of thirty–seven seemed
absurdly old, and sexless in a way. I ignored the pass, and
he never made another, though after I'd become
comfortable with him, I decided I would allow him to
seduce me if the occasion ever arose again. But it didn't. He
would sometimes talk of sex and beauty – my beauty in
particular – and he would catalogue my attractive features,
sometimes, telling me I had beautiful hands and eyes and
ears and legs and so on. But he never tried to turn it into
sex, or at least not at first, and then later when Malcolm
was on the scene I made it clear that I wasn't prepared to
be unfaithful. He respected that, I think, though sometimes
it was awkward when Malcolm and I went to see him as a
couple.

After we'd both been to dinner with him once or
twice, he asked me to come alone in future. Malcolm told
me that we should either go as a couple or not at all. He
disliked Richard and distrusted his motives, and he let it
show. But I had come to feel proprietorial about those

dinners. Besides, when Malcolm was there, Richard couldn't talk to me in the sensual way that had become our elegant secret.

Richard was somewhat taller than me and had a slight stoop, which wasn't apparent except when he was standing side on, and which made him seem ultra intellectual, somehow. It heightened the impression that he was trying to see things from my own perspective and caused him to appear almost predatory when in conversation face to face. He had an air of strength about him, too, and lively eyes, and an intense way of following my line of argument that was both expressive and validating. His large hands belied his resolute expression with their nervous, manneristic twitching – he had a way of constantly plucking at the seam of his trousers that made me want to grab his fingers and hold them tightly until they had stopped their furtive motion.

The most attractive aspect of Richard, I think, was the earnest attention that he paid to me. It was the first time a member of an older generation had ever treated me as an equal, and my involuntary response – over a period of time – was to allow our age difference to become irrelevant. His face, deeply lined for a man of his age, seemed to have become so through the habit of frowning with the intensity of his concentration. This made me feel a certain respect for him that went beyond the demands of his status. As faces go, his was really quite beautiful – a fact that I hadn't even registered at first, but which became more and more apparent as I began to interact with him as a person rather than an academic.

I should have guessed that Malcolm would become jealous; possessive and sulky. I was naive enough to think that just because Richard and I didn't stick our penises into each other that we weren't having a sexual relationship. Of course we were having a sexual relationship – or a *sensual* relationship at least. Malcolm was foul about it, and I ended up being sly because I wasn't prepared to give up those dinners.

When we were in the build–up to our finals and both

immensely busy, Malcolm and I decided to spend an evening together not studying. We arranged to go into town to get drunk and go on to New York, New York to dance. We hadn't been out for a couple of months and felt we were becoming boring. We arranged this some days in advance but, because I was so absorbed, I forgot. Richard invited me over on the evening I was supposed to be going out with Malcolm, and I accepted.

It hadn't even been a particularly brilliant evening with Richard. I'd been too preoccupied to relax and had ended up making excuses at eleven or so and had gone back to my room, only to find Malcolm lying on my bed, furious. He asked me where I'd been and I told him I'd had a meal with Richard. It was only then that I remembered about our previous arrangement.

I sat on the edge of the bed and put my head in my hands and said, `Oh, god I'm sorry,' knowing as I said it that the words were inadequate. Malcolm lay on the bed and looked at the ceiling and said quietly, `You fucker. You bastard. I've been waiting here all evening.'

I explained that I'd forgotten, but of course that was no excuse. *Why* I'd forgotten was what preoccupied him. `Just sod off back to Richard,' he told me, `he'll be happy to sleep with you. I thought we'd planned to do that ourselves, tonight, but I find I'm suddenly incredibly unrandy.'

I lay beside him on the bed and kissed him and told him that I loved him and that I didn't love Richard; that Richard posed no threat to our relationship. And he said, `Don't be so stupid, Ben, don't be so ingenuous. You're infatuated with the man. You only have to see the two of you together to see that you're both besotted.'

`No,' I said, `no, you're just being petty and jealous.'

`What's weird,' he went on, ignoring me, `is that you've never done anything about it. Not that Richard wouldn't jump at the chance to stick his dick in you if you would only let him. And I suppose you will, eventually. It's inevitable.'

And then I hit him. Considering we were so close on that

28

narrow bed, I hit him incredibly hard. I caught the ridge of his forehead, above his eyebrow, and his neck made a curious snapping sound as he fell backwards off the bed and onto the floor. He lay there unmoving for a few moments and I thought, briefly, that I'd killed him. I leaned over the bed and whispered, `Malcolm?' And then I noticed that his shoulders were trembling, a tremor was passing through his muscles – a tremor that grew in intensity until he was shaking.

I lay back on the bed and squeezed my eyes shut and wondered how it was possible that I could destroy everything that was important in my life. I had somehow nullified both my love for Malcolm and my friendship with Richard by reducing it to the absurd level of physical violence. And of course, by reacting in the way I had to Malcolm's assertion that I was infatuated with Richard proved, at least partially, that he was right. *I love him*, I thought, meaning Richard. I rolled the concept round my mind and found that it sounded entirely plausible. *I love him*, I thought, meaning Malcolm, and found myself giving a different but equally intense emotional response.

I guess Malcolm must have been right when he called me ingenuous. I hadn't even realised that it was possible to love two people at once. I had always imagined that there was platonic love and sexual love and that sexual love always felt the same and only happened with one person at a time. Of course I loved Richard. Of course I wanted to make love to him. The fact that I hadn't allowed it to happen, and would never allow it to happen for as long as I was with Malcolm, didn't mean I didn't want it.

Malcolm was still on the floor, so I leaned over the edge of the bed again. He was still shaking but had rolled over onto his back and I realised that he was laughing. He was lying there shaking with laughter.

`Ben,' he whispered at my startled face, `Ben.'

And then I felt the tears. They were caused by the knowledge that I was conducting my emotional life for myself only, without regard for others. In order to survive I had to give. In order to give I had to be prepared to be hurt.

Malcolm stopped laughing and got up to lie on the bed with me.

`It's okay,' he whispered. `It's okay.'

The next time I saw Richard I recounted this story to him and admitted that I loved both him and Malcolm. He seemed gratified and solemn and took me in his arms and kissed me. He kissed my cheeks, my eyes, my forehead, my neck, my fingers and my lips. I kissed him back, carefully, until he broke away.

`In a way,' he said, `you've destroyed what I liked about you most. The fact of your childlike trust in the simplicity of human relationships.'

I knew that he was, to some extent at least, teasing me by saying this, but that was very much his style. He had always trivialised the undoubted attraction between us – trivialised it in a way that proved its consequence.

`Do you want to have an affair?' he asked.

`I can't,' I said.

`I've enjoyed this while it lasted,' he said, `but things have changed. You must decide what you want to do. You can stay with Malcolm, be faithful to him, and stop seeing me; you can stay with him and have an affair with me, either with or without his consent, or you can leave him and have a relationship with me.'

`But why can't we go on like before?'

`You know why. It's gone too far, Ben, for friendship to be enough.'

He hugged me then and I could feel his erection pressed against my thigh, and I felt suddenly angry.

`Why?' I shouted. `Why do I have to choose? Why must everything always have to change?'

EIGHT
MALCOLM

I am sitting here with a photo of Ben. In the picture it is Christmas, our first Christmas together. He is sitting cross-legged in front of the tree, hands clasped in front of him as if in prayer. He has a deadpan expression, though when I look a little closer I can detect a wry humour and perhaps a touch of smugness. His hair is long, for him, and swept back with gel. He is wearing red trainers, faded blue jeans with a serious rip below the knee, and a brand new blue T-shirt – a present from his mother. He has a short, straight nose, a round chin that contrasts with his narrow cheeks. His eyebrows are substantially darker than his hair and his forehead already has two discernable worry lines. Behind him, under the tree, are a box of Quality Street, a gift pack of Cadbury's Flakes, an Osmiroid calligraphy set, some recycled stationery, a pair of Walt Disney boxer shorts and a bottle of champagne – given by my parents. The flash on the camera is too bright and too close which gives the picture a washed out, unreal quality, like memories from childhood. What is clear, though, is the happiness in his face, the contentment. He looks impossibly lean and elegant and guilelessly beautiful. I look at the picture and wonder at the destructive nature of curiosity – wonder why I ever let myself give Tag so much as a passing glance.

* * * * *

Having had sex with Tag, I found myself suddenly shy with him, which was a new emotion for me. I felt almost incapacitated by timidity as I walked over to his place the following day. Ben was at home trying to cope with a load of work that had suddenly come in, so it was as well for me to be out of the way. As I walked, I mused about how sex was supposed to bring people together. But it had made Tag more difficult to understand because he had been so selfish, I thought, with my body, and I wanted to ask him why he'd been that way. When I saw him, though, I couldn't bring myself to raise the subject. It was there

31

between us, and because it was there, it was difficult to talk of other things.

I looked at him and realised that he, too, had a secret – a secret which had hung between us that first day at the check-out, and which had attracted me to him. I was attracted to the mystery of his secret, just as I had been attracted to Ben's, two-and-a-half years before.

Tag suggested that we go for a coffee and lent me a scarf because there was a stinging chill in the light breeze. We walked from his place over to the café on the far side of the park and sat for a while at the window, squinting at each other in the brightness of the late-winter sun. Then he asked me about my past. It was the first time he'd asked a question about my life. I told him something about my liberal family in Halifax; my sister and brother; my acceptant parents. But now that Tag was being more gentle, I preferred to ask him a few questions about himself. I asked why he'd come to Manchester if he didn't know anyone here.

`Um,' he said. `Yes, Manchester. Why did I come here? Why not? It's a lively city. It's kind of brash and seedy and Chorlton is an okay part of it. Why did you come to Manchester?'

`I was at university here.'

`Yes, I know, but why did you stay?'

`For the reasons you've just mentioned, plus the fact that Ben and I have a lot of friends here.'

`Ah, friends . . . '

`We should introduce you around,' I said. `You may not like them, but at least it'll be a start for you.'

`Thanks,' he said. `Thanks, I'd like that.'

That's when I thought of having a party. We'd never had a party before, Ben and I, and we had already started sinking without a trace into the oblivion of poverty. It would be good for us to reacquaint ourselves with our friends, as well as to introduce them to Tag who was sitting in front of me, smiling, enigmatic – and suddenly I was absolutely unsure of his motives in being friendly with me at all; was unsure if he even liked me.

It occurred to me then that friendship is a curious thing. How is it that with some people you have worked your way into the very inside of their lives within minutes of meeting them, and with others, despite a great tenderness, you will always be strangers? Tag had spoken of the circumstances of his life, his travels, his lovers, but somehow his stories were edited to exclude himself – like family photos with the central figure cut from the print so that they show only as an absence.

`Come on,' said Tag, `let's go back to my place and jump into bed.'

`No,' I said, `it's not fair on Ben.'

`You said he'd told you it was okay.'

`That was for last night.'

`Come on.'

`I don't know if I can trust you,' I said. `In bed, I mean.'

Tag laughed and patted my hand.

`Don't worry,' he said, `I'll stay safely within your bounds.'

He smiled his overpowering smile and I was at once repelled by his assumption that I should want to repeat our less than satisfactory sexual encounter, and attracted by his monumental self-assurance.

We stood and I pulled the scarf tighter round my neck feeling unprepared and slightly disbelieving that this was the same person as the man who had been so impersonal with me the previous evening.

`Look,' said Tag, `I realise I overdid it when we went to bed last time and I'm sorry if I scared you. You're the best-looking guy I've seen since I came to Manchester and I don't want to ruin what's between us. Please, come back to my place and I'll get it right this time.'

Looking at Tag, part of me wanted to leave, now, and go back to Ben, and part of me wanted to give him another chance.

`Come on,' he whispered urgently, with an eager smile.

As it happened, when I did go back to his place, it was like making love with another person. He was close, concerned, thoughtful, and though he had a wilful habit of

33

posturing to show off his body, he wasn't pushy or demanding. I found it confusing that Tag could be so different. It was as if one of his incarnations was a mask. It made me wonder which one was real – the concerned, gentle person, or the thrusting aggressive one. It seemed inconceivable that they could both be aspects of one individual.

He made coffee afterwards and we sat on the settee in the front room, leaning against each other and looking out at the sky, which was dimming now with the end of the afternoon. I sat there thinking that what had happened between us had been pleasant, even profound in a holiday romance sort of way, but it made me realise the importance of Ben. Tag was simply the personification of my wilful, constant, irrational need for more.

`Ben isn't right for you,' Tag said. `You're too much of an extrovert to be happy living with someone like him, even if you do love him. He's weird and you're both far too young to know what you want.'

When I left, Tag said thank you to me in a voice that, although he looked nonchalant, sounded strangely desperate. I walked up High Lane and realised that Tag had never mentioned current friends – it was as if he'd never had friends; only lovers.

Ben was bored when I got back. His commission was to put two full-length text book manuscripts onto disc in preparation for publication. It was basically a typing job, although the typescript he was working from was so full of edits and arrows and biro-written parentheses that it was often difficult to follow. He'd ground to a halt and was sipping coffee whilst reading Doris Lessing. He put the coffee down and came over to me, reaching his arms round my waist and kissing me.

`Hi,' he said, `did you have a good walk?'

`Mmm,' I said non-committally.

`I'm running a bath. Come and join me.'

I knew that baths in the afternoon were a precursor to sex and felt my heart sink at the prospect of trying to pretend I hadn't already had an orgasm with Tag. I got into the bath, feeling torpid, and washed in a desultory way, and afterwards went through to the bedroom with Ben, where we made love for a long time. Ben seemed intense and alive after the tedium of his typing. He seemed so open with me, and spontaneous, that I found myself gagging when I thought of Tag. It took me a long time to come, and afterwards I hugged Ben without speaking.

NINE
TAG

I was born in the countryside of West Yorkshire, between the village of Oxenhope and the town of Hebden Bridge. My father had a small farm which he managed with single-minded zeal and great efficiency. My mother always hated being a farmer's wife and even though we had a pretty high standard of living by local standards, she still found it demeaning. She was a woman who wanted great things, but had very little idea about how to get them.

She wanted me to have an aristocratic name and, after some furious rows with my father, finally managed to have me christened Tobias Henry Winston Whitburn. My parents called me Toby, which I hated. My school friends called me Tag, which I liked, and when I moved to another school, I took the name with me.

My childhood was an obstacle to be overcome. My parents hated each other with an intensity that overshadowed everything else in my life. I became increasingly unhappy at home because my parents argued all the time, and if I was ever there at the wrong moment, I'd get it in the neck, from both of them, but especially my mother. I had no control or ability to make them stop.

My father was killed in a shooting accident when I was eleven. It caused a sensation in the village. It was assumed to be suicide, though the circumstances surrounding his death were inconclusive. He was found out on Hardcastle Crags. His shotgun was later recovered from the river, sixty feet below, thrown in some involuntary spasm, perhaps, after he'd pulled the trigger. When I was twenty-six my mother died, too, but before she did, she admitted that she had driven him to it – had as good as murdered him. I had always blamed her for the suicide, just as she did herself – there was something guilt-ridden about her and the way she talked of my father. She had a nervousness around the subject of death, and a way of praying in code that, in spite of her secrecy, allowed me to glimpse her feelings of guilt. I had often wondered about my mother; about her unhappiness and her obsession with sin and punishment. She had become very religious after my father's death, but it did no good because she died racked with guilt, just as she had lived. Regretting her husband's death had solved nothing. After a period of helplessness she'd sold the farm and used some of the money to buy into a newsagent business in Mytholmroyd with another widowed friend. It didn't make her happy. She replaced one brand of unhappiness with another. If I learned anything from my mother it was that you should never regret anything that you do. You should face the consequences of your actions and get on with your life.

I wanted to be strong, and so began my lifelong obsession with weightlifting. I hoped that physical strength would somehow cause a parallel emotional strength.

I studied engineering at Edinburgh University. By the beginning of my first year, I knew I was gay. I had one or two disastrous relationships whilst studying – one with a narcissistic and somewhat violent bodybuilder – and this eventually soured the city for me. After graduation I spent a long summer of indecision, then left Scotland for Somerset where I got a job with Westland Helicopters in Yeovil. I hated it. I'd thought aircraft were glamorous, but the industry was faceless, and the only chance of promotion was into dead men's shoes – and the threat of redundancy seemed to hover around us like the aircraft we were building. A lover of mine at the time told me that ecology was the skill of the future and I believed him and we went off together to work as unskilled labour on a project on the Severn Estuary. We fell out over a third party and he did not complete the project.

After that I moved to Bristol, where I got a job at a dental laboratory. Whilst I was there I met and moved in with a science teacher. We got on okay for a bit, but I couldn't be faithful to him because he was strangely undemanding. I began to see people on the sly and he followed me one night and smashed a bottle into the face of the guy I was with, causing two gashes that needed eleven and thirteen stitches respectively. I broke every window in his house whilst he was out and pissed off with all the money from our joint account. I figured he deserved everything he got.

I went to London where I moved in with an old friend from

Bradford who was reselling stolen goods and dealing in drugs. He put me up for a while, but someone ratted on him and the police trashed the apartment and took him away. I stayed on for a while amongst the debris, and kept my eyes open for opportunities.

I managed to bump into an acquaintance of my mother's who was running a recruitment firm in London dealing with career opportunities abroad. She set me up with a minor post in the French Institute of Agriculture in Lyon. They wanted people with engineering experience for various projects in the Massif Central and the French Alps. By this time I was receiving threats from my drug dealer friend's acquaintances, so it was a good time for me to move on.

Once settled in France, I got into the gay dinner party set, which was entertaining at least, if over bitchy. I went to the gym three times a week and slept around, which became monotonous after a while because the whole scene was so genteel and false, and no one would go for what they really wanted, being too busy drinking or camping it up over coffee in town on a Saturday morning. I pretty soon graduated to rougher types, and even rent boys occasionally. Sometimes I would overstep the mark with one of my tricks, but it was only because I felt I had to push them to their limits. This gave me something of a bad name, so I decided, once more, that it was time to move on.

I moved back to London where I stayed in Earls Court and met a bunch of wandering Australians. They were lively, brash and taught me quite a bit about aggressive sex. They moved on before long and I met this guy, Andy, who ran a successful antiques shop in Camden. He was the same age as me – thirty-three – and he was loaded. He had five properties in London, four of which he rented out. I worked for him in the shop for a year or so, and learned at least the rudiments of the trade. We became lovers and it was good at first, but because he was rich, he began to act like he owned me. One day I represented him at an auction in Wiltshire and I picked up a real bargain – an early Arnold Blackley. I didn't mention it to Andy and paid for it with my own money, flogging it in London when I got back and making several thousand on it. Andy heard about it and we had a real scene. I had bought a video camera which we used to make

38

movies of us fucking, and he threw it into the toilet, even though the whole thing had been his idea in the first place and I had paid for the camcorder. I didn't lay a finger on him, but packed a bag and left, taking a room in a seedy hotel in Battersea.

After that I dabbled on the scene. I went to a couple of leather bars, but I didn't like them. I hated being surrounded by aggressive-looking people. I wanted to be the only one. I wanted to be the centre of attention. I went back to the hotel and realised that most people in this world are wimps who have never experienced anything in their lives worse than acne.

A few weeks later I was reading THE PINK PAPER and saw an ad for a flat to rent in Chorlton, Manchester. I went for it, got it, and moved in straight away. I had several thousand in the bank and a certain amount invested in the Channel Islands from when my mother died, so I decided to look around before settling on what type of work to do.

Then I met Malcolm. He had a kind of vulnerable/hard look about him, as though he was afraid of being bruised but wanting it to happen all the same. And I thought, YES!

TEN
BEN

I knew that Malcolm was preoccupied when we were in the bath together. He had that `I'm not really here' expression and he didn't get an erection when I washed his back. In bed, when we made love, he closed his eyes which was also unusual, and it made me feel excluded. I made love carefully that day and enjoyed it less than I'd hoped, because I was held back by Malcolm's reserve. I thought of him making love with you the night before and wondered, as he lay there accepting my caresses, which one of us he was picturing. I wondered, too, about my mother and how my father must have felt when he realised that she was being unfaithful to him. Did he feel an overwhelming love for her, or a raging sense of betrayal?

I knew Malcolm hadn't been unfaithful to me, because I had given him permission to go and see you, but my rational acceptance of what had happened was confused by Malcolm's apparent emptiness now. I felt a curiosity and a sudden wash of sadness at the thought that I was losing control – that I had never had any control; that my relationship with Malcolm had been a precarious coupling that had lasted only as long as there was no outside influence.

Was that why I had tried so hard to close us off, to hermetically seal us against the outside world? I couldn't blame you for making a pass at Malcolm, nor could I blame Malcolm for giving in. But I needed to condemn someone and so I found fault with myself. I had driven Malcolm into your arms by clinging to him.

The following day Malcolm suggested that we have a party to introduce you to our friends. I felt something slipping within me as he said this, but we had seen so few people in the previous months that I couldn't say it was a bad idea. I just didn't want you to be there, that's all.

`It won't cost much,' Malcolm told me. `Just the price of a few snacks. We can tell everyone to bring their own drink.'

So we agreed a date. You came round for coffee that afternoon and stood in the kitchen with Malcolm, talking quietly, whilst he put the kettle on. Malcolm, as he conversed, laughed in a way that I had never heard before and I felt a sudden desperate surge of self-pity. What did I have that could compete with your self-assured, slick manoeuvring?

You came through with the coffee, still laughing at something Malcolm had said, and slipped your arm round my shoulder to pat me as though I were a pet. You absently handed me a mug, not looking at me, head turned to reply to Malcolm.

`Or a sauna . . . Manchester needs a decent sauna in the city centre. Maybe that's a good way to get faggots to part with their money.'

`What's this?' I asked.

`Tag's thinking of setting up in business. He's got some investments that he'd like to do something with.'

`I've got to decide where to go, and what to do,' you said, `and I still haven't decided whether to buy a place here or not. Maybe I should settle down and become a businessman.'

You smiled at me, then, a pleasant enough smile on the surface, but your eyes were cool and their message was clear: `Why don't you just fuck off and leave us alone'. It was the first time I'd felt your naked hostility towards me, and it shocked me because I'd never done anything to make you dislike me. I'd accommodated your place in my life with Malcolm, and although we still had to sort out what that meant, I think I'd been extremely tolerant.

You looked at me, and smiled, and said in your smarmiest, most insincere voice, `Do you fancy coming down to Cruz tonight? I haven't been for a week or two, and I've never seen you two down there, except for that first night.'

I shrugged and gave Malcolm a `there's nothing I'd like to do less' look, which he deliberately misread before accepting for both of us. After you'd left I looked at him, feeling hurt, and said, `You knew I didn't want to go,' and

41

he said, `Grow up, Ben. Come out and enjoy yourself. Tag's going to help us open up our lives. It's what we both need.' But I thought: there's change and there's change. This definitely did not sound like change for the better.

As we were getting ready to go out I realised that Malcolm was taking extra care getting ready – pulling out his most sexy jeans, putting in his gold earring, gelling his hair into the dinky tuft that I love but which I'd noticed drove you bananas. I realised that he was doing all this for you. I realised too that I was also dressing as smart and sexy as possible. So that I looked worthy of Malcolm? So that I attracted you? Because in some psychological way I was looking at you as a rival for Malcolm's attention?

We went down to Cruz and I got pissed, which I hadn't meant to do. I couldn't be indifferent to your intimacy with Malcolm. The fact that you'd slept with each other meant you had a connection which excluded me on such a profound level that I found it difficult to interact with you in anything but the most basic way. You casually draped your arm across Malcolm's shoulder and shouted in his ear every now and then, causing him to smile. Malcolm was aware of my exclusion and would pat my arm from time to time, but I could see that he was caught up in his new experience and even when he talked to me, I knew he wasn't thinking of me.

I danced with Malcolm a couple of times. You refused to join us, saying that you never danced. You stood on the edge of the dancefloor and watched for a while, and then wandered off downstairs to see who was around. It turned out that a number of regulars from your gym came down here, wearing vests and torn Levi 501s, or military style shirts and leather jackets. Malcolm was smitten by the thought of all that muscle and it didn't surprise me to find that you had persuaded him to go along for a preliminary session the following week.

I loved Malcolm's body as it was. I couldn't bear the thought of it becoming distended and pumped up through prolonged weight training. You were a borderline case for me, muscle-wise. You were tall, which meant you didn't look nearly as overdeveloped as some of those you stopped to talk to, but nevertheless, I think you would have looked better if you were leaner.

I went to buy us some drinks at around one a.m. I stood discreetly to one side of the bar and watched you and Malcolm together. You looked like an established couple standing there, so close to each other, watching the dancefloor. After a while, Malcolm looked around to see where I was. You followed suit and caught my eye almost immediately, giving me a sneering smile that was chillingly barbed. I nodded to you and, picking up our drinks, I took them over. Malcolm glanced from me to you and then back again. I think he felt, then, the frisson between us and he hugged me suddenly as if trying to deny to himself that he had noticed. I thought, *I must be strong – I must do the right thing, and that might mean doing nothing at all.*

You were too brash for Malcolm, too unsubtle for it to be serious or long-term. Okay, you were good-looking, but in a pale way that Malcolm would tire of. He was enjoying your surplus energy and had yet to be exposed to the aggression that I could already sense lurking beneath your smile. I just had to stand back and let it burn out. I just had to stand back and have another drink, and wear my anger away to the music, and wait.

ELEVEN
MALCOLM

I could see that Ben was desperately unhappy about Tag, but he wasn't going to say anything. When we were getting ready to go out, he put on his best party clothes as if to say to Tag, `This is what you have to contend with.' He looked good, too, in white jeans and a thinly striped canvas shirt with small pink-triangle studs on the tips of the collar, and, later, when I glanced at him – especially when he was dancing – I felt a fresh yearning for his body. Yet I was also aware that it was Tag's presence that highlighted my feelings for Ben. It was the danger that Tag represented which made what I had with Ben seem precious – because he made it seem so fragile. Still, there's no point denying that every time Tag smiled at me, or ran his finger across my thigh, I felt my dick stir.

There was one point in the evening when things got difficult. Ben made a mild statement about not finding over-developed bodies attractive, and Tag leant over to him and said something I didn't quite catch about wimps always being intimidated by muscle. Ben looked as though he'd been slapped across the face and wandered off on the pretext of buying some more drinks. I turned to Tag and asked him why he felt so antagonistic towards Ben, and he said, `You don't see it, do you? That boy is dragging you down into some kind of wishy-washy relationship where you're both going to die of terminal boredom. What are you doing with your life, Malcolm? You say you want a job, but you don't seem to be looking all that hard. You're just wallowing in pathetic inertia with a guy who's becoming a glorified typist. Wake up and take responsibility for making something of your life.'

This tirade was uncomfortable, not least because Tag was right about my lack of motivation in looking for a job. But he was wrong about Ben. I could see that it was just that Ben was in the way as far as he was concerned.

As soon as Ben was out of sight, Tag took my hand and

44

placed it on his crotch so that I could feel his hard-on. He leaned across and ran his tongue down my sideburn, then placed his hand on my crotch, on my hard-on.

`See,' he said.

Even whilst I found this sexy, I also found it slightly sick. I felt clandestine and randy and completely out of context. There was something peculiarly compelling about Tag, yet totally insubstantial, as though he would cease to exist once a mutual orgasm had been achieved. I looked over at the mirrored wall and saw us, standing close together, and it seemed as if we were navigating a sea of trivia that was masquerading as something important. I pulled away from Tag and felt that he had become a malignancy within me, and I thought, *Once I've introduced him to other people he'll be less intense with me.*

I could, of course, have told him to leave me alone, right then. But I fascinated him, and this fascination beguiled me. I was enjoying being the object of his attention and wanted to explore that feeling further to see where, if anywhere, the motivation for his attraction lay. I'd realised early on that Tag was a very closed person, and now I wanted to know in what way I fitted into his plans for the future. I also wanted an answer about where Ben and I were going with each other. Whilst I loved Ben and wanted to stay with him, there's no doubt I wanted our lives to change – to open up to the outside world; to reaccommodate our friends. For as long as I couldn't see how best to make change occur, then Tag had a purpose, because he thrust change upon us.

Tag's antipathy to Ben was hard, because the more alienated Ben became the more difficult it would be to sustain even a platonic relationship with Tag, who was by now becoming a fixation with me, if not an obsession. I knew it was a risk to go any further with him, but felt that right now the risk was worth taking. I'd have to act as mediator, that was all. I felt that they could learn from each other and that it was worth building a mutual respect between them, at least.

Then I thought of our party. As I stood by the dancefloor

watching Ben weaving his unsteady way back to us with our drinks, I felt a flutter of unwelcome anticipation. Tag had a look of such indifference to Ben that it was hard to be bright in their company without it seeming like the most appalling hypocrisy.

Another thing that worried me was that Richard was going to be present at the party. He'd been invited by Ben and had accepted. I didn't know how I would feel about seeing him again – especially in the knowledge that I had scuppered his intimacy with Ben, whilst Ben had allowed mine with Tag. Perhaps I would feel like a two-faced shit. Perhaps that's what I was.

TWELVE
' TAG

I went to the party with a certain anticipation. Whilst I wouldn't describe myself as shy, I do find it difficult to meet people in situations that aren't purely sexual; and though I didn't hold out any great hope of meeting anyone really worth knowing at Malcolm and Ben's place, at least it was a start.

I'd had a pretty naff evening at Cruz the night before, although I managed a grope with Malcolm at one stage, and a quick, hard kiss before we left. He dances well and I complimented him on it, saying that you could see how good he was in bed by the way he moved on the dancefloor. I knew that would get him, and it did. He kind of blushed and beamed and virtually purred when I told him I was looking forward to having sex with him again. But Ben had been in the way and I despised him for it. He danced well, too, but it didn't make me want to seduce him. On the contrary, he looked too graceful, really. Camp almost. Well okay, not camp, but kind of like a professional, with slick moves and so on, where I like to see well handled masculine sex language.

Malcolm told me about Ben's brother drowning and it made me hate him even more. Life isn't easy and to still be blighted by something that happened when he was three, Christ, how pathetic can you get? I showed him I disliked him, too. There's no point in being kind.

I turned up for the party with a bottle of Chianti, which I handed over, and a half bottle of tequila which I kept in the pocket of my flying jacket. I kissed them both and Ben kind of froze as I kissed him on the lips, as though I had bad breath or something. Malcolm frowned at him furiously, which I pretended not to notice. Malcolm was looking incredibly humpy in jeans and a sweatshirt that had a rip below his pec just large enough to insert a couple of fingers – which I intended to do before too long. Ben was all in white looking very *Brideshead Revisited* and angular and

47

virginal as though he should go off to bed for his first ever wank. He looked about fifteen and kind of obscenely, off-puttingly angelic. He was with this older guy who padded after him all the time like a puppy or a devoted aunt. This was the guy, Richard, that Malcolm had mentioned to me, who looked so fucking intense I felt I'd need a PhD before I'd be allowed to even say hello to him. I could see why Malcolm found him so much of a threat – he and Ben were two of a kind. Malcolm would have been much better letting them go off to set up house together in a kind of children's-story-perfection that might drag on for a lifetime of sheer tedium.

`Look,' I told Malcolm, `you've just got to get rid of Ben,' and Malcolm sighed and looked annoyed with me, or perplexed with Ben, or something that I couldn't read. But I knew I'd stirred his doubts and I knew that if he looked hard enough he would find Ben lacking. Meanwhile, I was introduced to various indifferent ex-students and a couple of scene queens that even I'd seen around in the pubs. There was no one there who had half as much spunk as Malcolm, so after I'd established the general level of blandness around me, I gave up on them and devoted my attention to him.

It was easy to get Malcolm on his own because Ben was sitting next to Richard in the corner, deep in conversation. I would touch Malcolm whenever I started on a new topic, or laughed or made fun of him. I kept catching him looking across to Ben to see if he was noticing this. I thought it would do Ben good to see it, so I carried on.

People kept coming up to Malcolm to ask how things were, to ask how his job hunting was going, to complain that he'd dropped below the horizon of their lives. There was a lot of university nostalgia which I found sickly to the point of nausea – as if university had been the pinnacle, for all these people, of freedom and social intercourse.

Malcolm had to go off to talk to someone in whom I had no interest so I stood for a while on my own, drinking and being ignored by Ben. After a couple of minutes Richard got up and came over to shake my hand. Ben went off into the kitchen.

`Hello,' he said. `I'm Richard.'

`Yes,' I said, `I know.'

He had radically black hair that was thinning slightly, and a longish, strong face that might have been attractive if his body language hadn't been so pathetic. He stood there and clasped his hands as though desperately trying to ingratiate himself. I sneered inwardly and smiled my best condescending smile.

`I don't have any academic friends,' I said.

`Well,' he replied, `we're human beings like everyone else.' He said this with a superior smile that made me want to punch him very hard in the solar plexus to knock the wind out of him.

`I'm going to get another drink,' I told him and walked off to the kitchen. When I got there, Malcolm and Ben were standing on their own by the sink.

`For God's sake, Ben,' Malcolm was saying, `give him a chance. You may not like him, but I do. That must mean something.'

`Hear, hear,' I said from the doorway.

Ben looked up at me in a kind of hurt way and said nothing. Malcolm looked so embarrassed he had to turn away.

`Come on, Ben,' I said, going in to the kitchen and pouring myself a glass of wine, `don't feel threatened by me.'

`Why not?' he asked. `You are a threat.'

`Depends what you mean by threat.'

`What is it with you?' he asked. `You come stomping into our lives like some macho wanderer, but there's nothing you can do to hide the fact that you've come to Manchester because you've fucked up your life elsewhere. Why else set out to make this new start? I don't see any evidence of a single positive reason why you've come here. You've run away. You've always been running away, and you despise me because I've got nothing to run away from. You detest my stability and want to take it away from me. Your infatuation with Malcolm is nothing more than a

49

power game.

`I thought I was the one with attitude problems, but you're just a kid inside, a pathetic insecure kid who won't even admit he's fucked up. I feel sorry for you even as you're trying to ruin things between Malcolm and me.'

That was too much for me, the little shit. No one talks to me like that. In two strides I had him by the lapels and heaved him up against the wall. With one thrust I butted his head against the rough plasterwork hard enough to make him give a strangulated choke.

`Oh, great,' I said. `You know fuck all about my life, you creep.'

I pressed him to the wall and bashed his head against it with each word I spoke. `Do . . . you . . . think . . . I . . . give . . . a . . . flying . . . fuck . . . what . . . you . . . think . . . '

Someone grabbed my arms and, with surprising strength, pulled me away from Ben. It was Richard, breathing hard. Ben slumped against the table, blood coming from somewhere at the back of his head. Malcolm stood, speechless and motionless, watching us. I wondered if I should have a go at Richard for good measure but decided against it. I went into the hall, picked up my flying jacket, and left.

THIRTEEN
BEN

When I was twelve my mother went into a private hospital for some plastic surgery. There was a prominence at the bridge of her nose, and a downturn at the end, which made her feel like a freak from a Punch and Judy show. Actually, her nose was wasn't all that bad. It wasn't a great nose, but it wasn't the type of feature that people would immediately notice when meeting her.

She saved up for three years for the operation and was so excited when she went into the private clinic that even I thought it was a good idea. My stepfather put up half the money and they both thought it would mend their lives in some deep and permanent way.

When the bandages came off, my mother's face was swollen and discoloured, but the bump and the hook had gone. She was thrilled to the point of mania and spent a fortune on new clothes.

After four weeks something important moved inside and her nose swelled up frighteningly from her forehead to her upper lip, closing her eyes and puffing up her cheeks. She had to go in for emergency surgery which remedied the internal physical crisis, but left her with a permanent exterior thickening as though she was an alcoholic boxer. From then on she regarded herself as being irrevocably damaged. `Why?' she used to ask me, `why does everything always go wrong?'

It was years later that I discovered my stepfather had caused the failure of the nose-job by punching her whilst drunk. He let this fact slip one evening when they were arguing about whether I should stay on at school or go out to work. My stepfather wanted me out of the house. My mother wanted me to be a success.

`A success,' he sneered, `a success? Since when has anything round here been a success?'

At this, my mother burst into tears in a way that was new to me then, but which was to become sadly familiar – a heavy sobbing that made her rock gently back and forth.

`Shut up,' he shouted, `bloody shut up!'

But she was incapable of shutting up, and carried on and it frightened me to see her like this, so utterly abject and beyond *comfort. My stepfather seemed to explode inside and raised his arm to strike her, but my mother put her hands to her face and screamed, 'No! No! Leave my face alone.' And then they both stopped and looked at me as though they were holding their breath, and I thought, YOU BASTARD!*

When I was at university, after I'd come out to them and had been told never to show my face again at home, my mother came to see me under the pretext of visiting her sister in Oldham. She cried and said she thought my lifestyle was wrong, but so long as I was happy that was all she cared about, and she said, 'Just don't end up like me, that's all.'

✳ ✳ ✳ ✳ ✳

The party was awful. I'd wondered if there was going to be a scene after you had been so frosty towards me the previous evening at Cruz, and of course I was right.

The evening started well. It was months since I'd seen Richard and it was extraordinary how there was an immediate connection between us – not sexual, particularly, but utterly intimate and secure and with an undertone of astonishment that we had drifted apart. I could read his smile of greeting perfectly. He was happy to meet me again, curious to see how I would relate to him after this sabbatical in our friendship, and open to the possibility of causing a certain amount of mischief.

I, on the other hand, felt a flutter of confusion about Malcolm. Richard was the person I had forfeited for Malcolm's sake, and talking to him made me question whether it had been worth it. My two years with Malcolm had been an intense respite from the rubble of my family life, but your presence made me feel that all bonds between people are frail, where before I had imagined that, at least sometimes, they might be unbreakable. I suppose life is full of preconceptions waiting to be dashed against the intransigence of experience, but I felt that I'd been cast adrift and the people who had caused this to happen were precisely the people with whom I couldn't discuss it.

I briefly mentioned you to Richard without going into

any details, but he was perceptive and he closely questioned me about you, and I couldn't really lie to him, though I didn't say much. He was interested and intrigued and I was pleased that he didn't seem to regard me as a potential lover any more. We ended up talking like good friends, which is what I guess we'd become.

I realised that evening that it was worth rekindling my relationship with Richard. As a friend he would be a more stable presence than as a potential lover – and I needed stability just then. He had a touch of cynicism to his humour, and a touch of roguery, so that, with him, it was difficult to get things out of perspective. And there was no problem in resuming our friendship. Malcolm could hardly object to me seeing Richard, given his situation with you, though merely thinking in this way seemed to highlight a gap between us. It was all a question of survival, in a sense. I had to survive you.

Richard went over to talk to you at one point, so I slipped into the kitchen to have a word with Malcolm. But Malcolm was drunk and angry. You had obviously been whispering offensive things about me, which did you no credit and Malcolm even less, since it seemed he'd listened to them. He asked me why I disliked you so much and I told him that, actually, contrary to appearances, I didn't dislike you at all. I was wary of you, yes, and mistrustful, but that wasn't the problem. It was your intense dislike of me which put paid to any cordiality between us. But Malcolm wouldn't accept this and blamed me for being unwilling to even try.

Then you were in the doorway listening to us and looking amused and pleased that we were having an argument. I looked straight into your eyes, then, and you saw my anger and you let me see that you were pleased that I was angry and hurt. And then you said you weren't trying to threaten my relationship with Malcolm, which was such a blatant insincerity that I exploded, which you weren't expecting and which shocked you even though you tried to hide it. The monumental insecurity that had caused your burning need to be destructive had become so obvious it amazed me that Malcolm couldn't see it.

And suddenly you went for me, grabbing me by the lapels and bashing me against the wall. Malcolm was transfixed and didn't know what to do, but Richard heard you shouting and came running in to grab you in an impromptu bear hug, pulling you back so that I could fall forward. You had half asphyxiated me and I stood there, dizzy for a few seconds, whilst you stomped out and the kitchen filled with concerned friends whose faces bobbed about in front of me as I felt the blood trickling down my neck. Richard led me over to the basin to help clear me up and shooed people from the room, and then took me through to the bathroom.

When I emerged ten minutes later with shaved patches at the back of my scalp where he'd dressed my cuts, the sitting room was empty except for Malcolm. `I guess that put a dampener on the evening,' I said, and smiled, but Malcolm was furious and hate-stared Richard and walked past us into the bedroom and slammed the door.

`Uh-oh,' Richard said, and hugged me.

FOURTEEN
MALCOLM

I had four lovers before I met Ben. Gary, when I was sixteen, who had great teeth and a constellation of spots from his temples to his throat. I liked him for this because I was spotty too, but less so than he was, which stopped me from feeling unduly self-conscious when I was with him. He was serious to the point of tedium, and though the sex was a revelation, we never had any fun.

Then there was Joe, who was physically similar to me and who was demonstrative and tactile and mischievous and who liked to wrestle with me in the shower and race me to the end of the road. He dazzled my parents, too, and they would go all smiley and breathless whenever he was round, and he'd flirt shamelessly with them, especially with dad, who used to laugh a lot. I was seventeen and Joe was nineteen. He was so vibrant it was amazing and I thought it would really go on for ever, but one evening when I came home early from swimming practice, I heard him crying in the kitchen. I stood outside the door and heard a buzz of voices – his and my father's.

I felt betrayed. I couldn't believe that Joe would confide in my father and not in me. I crept back outside and made a noisy, showy entrance to give them time to compose themselves. By the time I got into the kitchen my dad had his back to me, filling the kettle. `Coffee?' he asked. Joe looked startled and unhappy and left almost immediately. I followed him out to say goodbye, but he didn't kiss me, just looked at me and brushed my shoulder with his hand, as though to remove an excess of dust. `Why couldn't I have had a dad like yours?' he said.

I phoned him the next day, but he was distant with me and said he felt uncomfortable round at our house. I offered to meet him at his place, or on neutral ground, but he said, no, it wasn't working and, please, not to call him again. I realised, then, that he'd fallen in love with my father. A year or so later my dad told me about the kitchen episode and how he'd felt completely helpless in the face of Joe's infatuation, and mum said it was a shame that I'd lost such a good friend over something so hopelessly impossible.

And then there was Tim, who had a malleability about him that made him a great companion for a while, but who eventually bored me. I wanted someone who would disagree with me, or encourage me into new experiences, but Tim did neither of these things and the sex with him was flat and it petered out into nothingness. After we'd stopped seeing each other, whenever I bumped into him in the street I could think of absolutely nothing to say to him except hello.

Then there was Brian, in my first year at university. He was twenty-eight and worried my parents with his possessiveness. He wanted to delve inside me; to understand me and to own me. He'd always be asking me probing questions about how I was feeling. He was the first person who had taken the time and effort to really explore my personality and I was captivated by his interest in me. He took up so much of my time that my studies suffered. Eventually he had a minor breakdown, failed his first year, and left. He was the only person I'd met who had secrets that he wouldn't divulge. I never did get to know why he'd allowed himself to fail when he was so demonstrably bright, or why he left me without a word of explanation.

And then there was Ben.

* * * * *

I know I should have been sympathetic towards Ben, but I wasn't. I've never seen him go for anyone in the way he went for Tag. So much for Tag's assertion that Ben is wimpy; his was an impressive display of aggressive behaviour. I sort of admired him for it, whilst being furious that he could be so disruptive.

Of course I was shocked when Tag grabbed him like that and it's no excuse to say that he didn't realise the rough plasterwork was a hazard to Ben's skull. He shouldn't have done what he did. But then, Ben shouldn't have provoked him either.

After the first impact against the plaster I could see Ben's blood smearing the wall with each thump, like strange footprints appearing in snow. I just stood there and didn't know how to stop what was going on. Luckily Richard came in and broke it up, which was just as well because for a moment I really thought Tag was capable of killing Ben. Then Richard took over and ushered Ben through to the bathroom, leaving me on my own in the kitchen feeling useless and usurped because surely it was *my* responsibility to care for Ben?

This violence became a cue for a general exodus. Our guests were shocked and intrigued by what had happened, and I caught some smiles and nudges as they said their farewells. I went and sat in the sitting room and stretched my hands out, palm downwards, and thought, *What do I want? What do I really want?* And it annoyed me that I couldn't answer without qualification. Part of me wanted to express my incredulity at Tag; my shock that he could have been so violent, and another part of me felt let down that the flirtation I had envisaged for the evening hadn't come to anything. I was angry with Tag, but intrigued by him too, and wanted to work out why Ben's assertions had made him go berserk. There was something that he was hiding from and Ben, it seemed, had opened up an old wound. He had lit the relevant fuse and then, bang, Tag had exploded.

Later, I pretended to be asleep when Ben came to bed. I was still confused about him seeing Richard again, and looking so happy and relaxed in his company. Also, I didn't want to give him sympathy about his injured head because that would mean having to say sorry for being angry and uncommunicative earlier – but I was still angry and couldn't pretend that I wasn't.

He climbed in beside me and hugged me for a short while, gently disengaging himself so that he wouldn't wake me when he settled himself down to sleep. I lay there listening to his breathing and then turned towards him. In the darkness I could just make out the two shaved patches on the back of his head where Richard had dressed his cuts, and I felt an overwhelming desire to take the plasters off and wash the cuts and dress them again myself, to somehow have been the one who took charge when it happened. Instead I just lay there and thought, *I'm losing him.*

The way out of this is easy, I thought. *I just have to tell Tag to leave us alone.*

I lay and wondered why this was so rationally plausible and so emotionally impossible, and I came up with no answer as the hours passed. When I became aware of the stirrings of dawn – the washed out light behind the curtains and the chattering of starlings – I realised that I had lost a night's sleep over Tag. Previously I had only ever lost sleep over people as I was falling in love with them. I knew what my wakefulness implied, but couldn't bring myself to put a word to it. I didn't want to make it real.

In the morning I did hug Ben and apologise to him. I told him that I was pleased that Richard had come to the party and that they were friends again. He left after breakfast to go to the barber for a number one buzz-cut, to make his shaved patches less conspicuous, and when he came back he looked alien, naked, as though he'd just hatched from an egg. It made me realise what a beautiful face he had, with his large eyes and expressive mouth and high forehead. He had several bumps on his head, away from his cut, which made him look ravaged by life, and we laughed about them and he said he'd never make a convincing skinhead, and I said, `At least you've tried it and know it doesn't suit you,' and he laughed again and went off to buy himself a hat.

Whilst he was out Tag came round, which I thought was inappropriate and I told him so. I didn't invite him in, so we stood for a while talking on the doorstep. He said that I was his friend and if he wanted to come and see me then that was our affair and had nothing to do with Ben.

`Have you seen what you did to him?' I asked, horrified by his casual manner. He shrugged.

`I think you should sort out your attitude towards Ben,' I told him, `because for as long as we have a friendship, then Ben's going to be a part of that in one way or another because he's here, with me, and I want it to stay that way. Either you two can become friends or there's no future in this. Think about it.' And I closed the door.

Ben came back an hour or so later wearing a red felt cricketing cap with white piping. It made him look cute and sort of schoolboy-ruffian. He was carrying a bunch of flowers that had been left on the doorstep.

`For me, from Tag,' he said, handing me the little card of apology that came with them.

FIFTEEN
TAG

I used to love going to Scarborough – it was such a change from Hebden Bridge. My mother's sister lived in Sheffield and had a holiday cottage a few miles down the coast from Scarborough, at Filey Bay, which we would go and stay in during the holidays, when she wasn't renting it out. But by the time I was seventeen I hated being with my mother and my aunt. Mum was a widow and my aunt a spinster. They sat around all day talking about men and how awful they were, and how sullen I was, and how ungodly. I used to slip out for long walks on my own.

When I finished at university I told my mother I'd been invited down to Cornwall. I hadn't been asked at all, but wanted an excuse to remain up in Edinburgh whilst getting out of going to Scarborough.

I borrowed the flat of a couple of friends from university who had gone to India for six weeks, and took to cruising a lot round the castle and up by Calton Hill. Sometimes this could be dangerous, especially when it came to having sex in the dark with people I hadn't really seen; but I was reckless and unhappy and wanted something extreme to happen to me to counteract the deadly nothingness of my life to date.

One warm evening, when I had been wandering around, shirtless, leather jacket in hand, I went with this mean-looking guy who let me suck him off before demanding money. I actually had quite a lot of money on me, having cashed a cheque from my mother that afternoon, and I wasn't about to let him have it. Even when he pulled a knife, I refused to hand over my jacket. We stood there in the near darkness, staring at each other, and I was daring him, inwardly, to try, to just try something. And he did. He kind of spat, and lunged at me, swiping the knife across my front in a wide arc that bit deep along my chest. But he stumbled and I chopped his arm with the edge of my hand and he dropped the knife, and we scuffled for it. I reached it first and, without hesitation, I slipped it into him below his pec, where I guessed his heart would be. It went in with incredible ease and he went kind of stiff and murmured something that sounded almost loving, or orgasmic, before he slumped against me. I sat there bleeding, covered in his blood, and then stood slowly and walked away and sat looking out at the cityscape, ripping up handfuls of grass to wipe away the blood from my hands, chest and jacket. When I'd stopped bleeding so badly, I put on my jacket and made an attempt to saunter to my flat, which was just off Lauriston Place, on the south side. I was almost doubled up with pain and the need to hide the bleeding, so my sauntering must have looked kind of awkward, but I was feeling released from all the meaningless crap that I'd been submerged in all my life. I'd cleansed myself with pain.

I let myself into the flat and went straight to the bathroom where I washed myself again and put my bloodstained clothes in to soak and dressed my wound as best I could. I stayed out of sight for a couple of weeks, until I'd more or less healed. I wasn't worried about being caught for the murder. I knew the police wouldn't be particularly bothered about the death of such a low-life hard case. It only merited four lines in THE SCOTSMAN. I sat at home and decided that at the first opportunity I would leave for Hebden Bridge.

NOW MUM, I thought to myself, WE'VE BOTH KILLED SOMEONE. ONLY I DID IT PROPERLY.

✿ ✿ ✿ ✿ ✿

Leaving flowers for Ben was a bad idea because of the contrition that it implied. I didn't regret smashing his head against the wall. He deserved it and it had probably done him some good – woken him up to a bit of reality. But I decided to lie low for a while and then take it from there. Maybe I'd take them both out to Cruz and get them pissed and see what happened. Maybe I should have bashed Malcolm's head against the wall as well as Ben's, because they both needed a jolt.

In the meantime, I decided to go to London for a couple of days to get away from Manchester and the whole business. I went down and stayed in a guesthouse in Earls Court – my old haunt – that I found in a gay listing and went out for the night to the Brief Encounter and then on to

Comptons. I was kind of out of it and didn't feel like I was a part of the crowd. Maybe it was my mood, which was one of introspection – almost depression. I hate feeling like that and usually in the past have found myself recoursing to drugs to liven myself up. Now, though, there was no one I knew who could supply me, and I had to stick to alcohol, which was no friend in circumstances like these. I drank myself into a slow motion state of despondency and fell into a taxi shortly after eleven.

I spent the second day wandering around town and even went up to the Heath at one point and trolled round for a while looking for daytime trade. There was a time when I would have picked up any one of several men I saw there; but I looked at them and thought, *What is the point? Why bother?* No one I saw was in anywhere near as good shape as me, so I might just as well go back to my room and have a wank in front of the mirror.

Although I had no leather gear with me, I decided to go to the L.A. that evening because I was feeling angry with myself for moping about and wanted to do something to let off the steam that had started building. As soon as I walked in I saw Andy, sitting looking at the door. He was wearing jeans with leather chaps over them and a harness top under a black leather jacket. He'd never been particularly into that scene before, but it didn't surprise me to see him here. He'd always had a streak of attitude in him a mile wide, that had previously been hidden below the surface. I noticed from his exposed stomach how he'd already started going to seed. He smiled when he saw me, an unreadable smile that might have meant he was pleased to see me, but it might just as easily have meant that he was scared shitless.

`Hi,' he said, `you're in good shape.'

I nodded because I knew it was true, and I let him buy me a drink. He sighed and leant against me and asked me what I was doing, as though there had been no big scene between us, no terminal bust-up. I mentioned Manchester, but only in passing. Andy was part of my past, and I didn't want him cropping up on my doorstep.

`Come home with me,' he whispered after our second pint, and I accepted his offer, with certain reservations. But what else was there to do? He grabbed a taxi and we went back to his place – so familiar and so alien. He kept on saying what good times we'd had and shit like that, and when he'd got me a beer from the fridge, he took a video out and played it for me. It was of us fucking in the front room. It was atrocious quality, but there was something raunchy about it that made it look like a genuine porn movie.

`Number one box office, this one,' he said. `All my friends think you're incredible.'

We went through to the bedroom and I stripped. Andy kept his gear on and I played with his tits for a while, but I didn't get a hard-on. He had some straps and chains and let me tie him up, which was kind of fun and his *big* mistake. Once he was secure, I realised I could do anything I liked with him. I got on to the bed and stood on his diaphragm. This set him choking and crying out with pain, but I looked at him and said, `You're shit, Andy. What makes you think I'd want to have sex with you? Don't you remember what you did to me? What makes you think I want to have a fuck for old time's sake?'

He groaned at this and looked panicky. I took a whip and held it under his chin as he lay there on his back, legs splayed. I looked into his face and said, `But just to be nice – just for old times' sake, I *am* going to fuck you, and you're going to take it. I won't use a condom because I can't be bothered.' I reached over and picked up his tube of K-Y and covered his arse with the clear gel. I had a real hard-on by now and I brandished it in his face. `I never did take the test,' I told him. `Perhaps I've got it.' I lowered myself on top of him and slipped my dick into his arse. `Perhaps I've got it,' I whispered again, `and perhaps I'm going to give it to you.'

I fucked him and he twisted his face away from mine and bit against the pillow. I came almost immediately, which was irritating, and as I did so I was washed by an overwhelming sense of hatred for Andy. For Andy, and my mother, and the guy in Edinburgh that I killed; and for my father and Ben. I stood up and pulled some clothes on. Andy was obviously in pain, but I didn't give a shit. When I was dressed I stood on the bed and kicked him in the face with my doc. He kind of choked and lay there, blood smearing the pillow.

`Bye, Andy,' I said as I let myself out, `it was nice seeing you again.'

SIXTEEN
BEN

After the flowers arrived, you maintained a profound silence. Malcolm went round to your flat but there was no sign of you. I had mixed feelings about the apology, but was intrigued at the idea of seeing you again – having ignited the touch paper of your explosive home truths, I wanted to see if there was any interesting debris.

Malcolm was suddenly attentive again, and sociable, and he even suggested that I went to see Richard; which I did, spending a wonderful afternoon of conversation with him without the problem of innuendo cropping up once. Malcolm and I went round to a couple of old friends for a meal and wondered why we had allowed ourselves to get stuck in our internalised winter time warp.

I'd got myself another couple of textbook jobs from a small publisher and indexing specialist, and so I had a certain amount of disposable income – plus the prospect of regular future work if I wanted it, which I didn't really but at least it gave me a comfortable breathing space, career-wise. Malcolm had a couple of job interviews coming up, which seemed to hold an inevitability about them that was frighteningly obvious-next-step-in-life-ish.

Then you turned up unannounced nearly a week after the party and dragged us out for drinks and then on to Cruz. I knew you were finding it difficult to be cordial to me, but you made a passable attempt at sincerity which I pretended to believe was genuine. You drank a great deal and, by virtue of being in your company, we drank a lot too.

I danced on my own for a while; was joined later by Malcolm, and then finally by you. You gyrated in a most unusual manner. Having told me you never danced, I realised that something out of the ordinary was happening. Your half-closed eyes and intensity of expression seemed to be external signs of some internal transformation.

Afterwards, when we went to reclaim our drinks from the bar, you leaned between us and placed your unsteady arms over our shoulders. Head lolling forward, damp hair trailing into your eyes, you smiled, and by the pressure beneath your palm expressed a closeness that cut through all the earlier hours of pretence.

Malcolm excused himself and went off for a piss and you turned to me and whispered, `I can change. I *can* change.' You weren't saying it to me, but to yourself, and you looked as though you knew that, although you believed it with a passion right now, in the morning you would wake up to find yourself exactly the same – with neither the will nor the ability to do anything about it.

`Why were you so unpleasant to me at the party?' I asked you, feeling that now was perhaps the only opportunity for me to seriously pose this question.

`Your trouble,' you said, `is that you're too fucking perceptive. I've done some terrible things in my life, okay. I know that. I kind of want to do something to put that right – to make amends. But sometimes I look at people who have never done anything wrong and it looks to me like their lives are so anodyne, so *unlived* that I'd rather be a reprobate. I sometimes decide that I'll make a change, move somewhere and start again, and I meet yet another bunch of lifeless farts who act as if they're superior. It makes me mad – the fact that given the choice of living or not living, people choose to not live. It seems to me that pain is the only real way of knowing you're alive. Pain and unhappiness. And, while you might say that pain is unpleasant, there's one thing that it isn't, and that's boring.'

`There are other ways of experiencing life,' I said.

`Yes, but not that I've ever found. Maybe we just get what we deserve.'

I hugged him, and he enveloped me in his arms and kissed the top of my ear and said sorry and brushed the palm of his hand over my scalp.

`My fault I presume?'

I nodded and he leaned forward and kissed me on the lips, just as Malcolm arrived and put his arms around our waists.

`Well,' he said, smiling at us, `*well!*'

I smiled back, a little uncertainly, and for a moment I thought you were going to pull us into a triple embrace. For a second I saw a naked vulnerability in your face and what can only be described as a yearning for affection; I felt the start of the pressure from your arm, like an involuntary jerk, and then the moment passed and you laughed and offered us both another drink.

I stood and watched your broad back as you strolled off and wondered at the desperate nerve I had struck in you when I'd accused you of having fucked up your life. It made me shiver to remember the `help me' look that you'd given just as you kissed me, as though you were half drowned in some terrible karmic soup.

`What was all that?' Malcolm asked.

`I don't know.'

You came back carrying three pints and I had only taken a sip when you said, `Let's go home. The three of us, let's go back to my place.'

Malcolm looked at me with a subdued `yes?' in his eyes and I stood there feeling drunk and obscurely happy. Malcolm took my hand and turned to you.

`Okay,' he said, `but make it our place.'

This was so unexpected that, at first, I didn't fully comprehend what was going on. We left our drinks and wandered outside and along to the taxi rank. I was feeling trembly from a mixture of drunkenness, discovery (that you were somehow *human*) and released lust from fancying you for such a long time without having previously fully admitted it to myself. You lolled in the taxi, especially as it went round corners, so that you brushed against me occasionally in a half deliberate way, and kept glancing across and smiling. You were doing the same with Malcolm and I saw a flicker of complicity pass between you. Even so, despite the pretence of casualness, I could sense the tension in you, as though you were about to succumb to something of which you were terrified.

When we got back, this anxiety was even more notice-able, which I found strange – especially considering how drunk you were. Malcolm was the first to pull us into an embrace, in the hallway of the flat, and then he ushered us into the front room where you stood, shivering with tension. I suggested a massage and went to get the oil and an old blanket, and we all took our clothes off and you lay face down, with a cushion as a pillow, and Malcolm and I knelt on either side of you and massaged your back and legs and arms and arse. The knotted muscles were slow to relax, but they did so gradually, and Malcolm leaned across you and kissed me gently, his dick tumescent but no more.

It was quite extraordinary how sensual this scene was. My hands glided over your skin, over the ridges of muscle at your shoulderblades, and I realised then that Malcolm was the only person I had ever massaged, until now. Your alien flesh was secretive, yet yielding, and I could tell by your breathing that you were beginning to fall asleep.

Afterwards we showered briefly and crawled into bed, you in the middle, and I fell asleep almost immediately wondering about precisely what was happening to us, but not really caring – thinking how odd you were to find it so difficult to give in to your less aggressive side, and wondering what it was that made you shut it out. I wondered, too, as I drifted off, if the massage scene had been intimate enough to be termed sexual, and what that would mean for the three of us when we woke up . . .

When I did wake up, however, I had a hangover and a feeling that the light from the window, whose curtains we had failed to draw, was too pale to be quite natural. It seemed to pulse gently at the back of my eyes like a dull pain turned visible.

I rolled over gently and brushed Malcolm's arm with my own. You had gone. You had slipped out without our noticing and I felt certain that you had crept away out of embarrassment at showing us what you obviously thought of as a weakness. I lay there and felt a mixture of relief and sadness. Perhaps you would never be anything but mixed-up, and it was as well to have as little to do with you as possible. But nevertheless, there was a part of me – probably motivated by lust – that wanted to drag you back between us and make you succumb to some warmth.

SEVENTEEN
MALCOLM

I had wanted this to happen – for the three of us to go off together – but I hadn't discussed it and was surprised when Tag instigated it as he did at Cruz. After the previous week I'd had a certain feeling of confusion about what he thought of Ben, having bashed his head against the wall and then given him flowers. But I couldn't believe that he wanted to sleep with Ben; to have sex with him. It seemed such an inversion of everything he had said about him, about his wimpishness and his lack of gym-related physical credibility. But there was no denying the sincerity with which he'd suggested that we go back together. In fact it was almost shocking, the sudden display of his frightening *need*. Ben had somehow pulled a scary switch in him that had opened him up and shown a plaintively vulnerable side that I hadn't suspected was there. I was pleased, but wary of what Ben would think of the whole thing, and wondered whether he would feel that I had organised it all with Tag beforehand. Of course I hadn't – his suggestion was as much a surprise to me as it obviously had been to Ben.

When we'd got back to the flat we were far too drunk to have sex proper, so Ben's suggestion of a massage for Tag was a touch of genius. It helped bring down a few barriers between us, and made me feel close to Ben, and affectionate towards Tag in a new way. I was amazed at how life can come up with these surprises. Only a week ago I'd thought Tag had blown everything. I thought Ben would never want to see or speak to him again. But in a way, I realised, Tag's violence had become a terrible admission to Ben. Tag had let his insecurities be revealed and, once exposed, Ben's knowledge made him, somehow, a confidant. There was certainly a complex dynamic there and though I could sense a definite bond springing up between them, I couldn't yet judge its significance or its direction.

When I woke up in the morning to find that Tag had gone, I felt let down by him, deflated. I suppose it stopped there being any morning-after awkwardness, but the question mark that he left instead was far harder to interpret. Ben said nothing, but smiled and cuddled me and didn't refer to the previous evening except to mention his hangover. I made us coffee and toast and brought it back to bed and we whiled away the morning until Ben got up to do some work.

I pottered around the flat for a while and then went out for a walk. Of course I went straight round to Tag's, where he seemed to be expecting me. He let me in and made us some coffee.

`Why didn't you stay?' I asked him.

`I don't often make mistakes,' he replied, `but that was one of them – going back with the two of you. I don't even fancy Ben, for Christ's sake. He gives me the heebies, as it happens, and he's kind of gaunt without his clothes on, and I only let the whole thing happen because I was drunk.'

`But you were the one who suggested it,' I pointed out.

This seemed to nonplus him and he shrugged slightly.

`That kid really freaks me out,' he said. `I shouldn't have gone for him at your party, but he talks to me as though he's looking right into me.'

It was the first time I'd heard Ben referred to as a kid, and it made me realise how young we both were and how inexperienced in dealing with circumstances like these.

`Look,' he said. `Now we're here, let's finish off what we should have done last night.'

He came over and put his arms round me and hugged me hard.

`No,' I said, pulling away. `We've got to sort this out. I can't go to bed with you until we've sorted out about Ben.'

`Forget Ben,' said Tag. `Right now, he's irrelevant.'

`No. Either I want you to involve him in some way, or this whole thing has got to stop.'

`What's got to stop, our friendship? Our having sex?'

`Both.'

`What do you want me to do, give Ben a charity fuck?'

`That's not how I would describe it.'

`Okay, okay,' he raised his arm. `I'll think about it.'

`Your problem,' I said, `is that you can't accept how wise Ben is. Now that you see he's got the measure of you, you find him intimidating. Don't. Maybe just by knowing him you'll find that he's your first real chance to make a fresh start. We've got a lot to offer, Tag, we both have. Don't be all macho and aggressively cut off. Give a little.'

`I'll think about it,' he said. `Now just fuck off for a while, alright? I want to be on my own.'

I left his flat and walked slowly home. Why did I want to include Tag in my relationship with Ben? Because I fancied him? I fancy lots of people but that doesn't make me want to include them in my life. (And did I fancy him, anyway? I wasn't even sure about *that*.) The thing was that sex with Tag seemed so instructive, so much more electrifying, so *dangerous* in comparison to anything I'd experienced before. Also, being bored with my life on the dole made me that much more capable of taking extreme decisions.

Anyway, my motivation was going to be put to the test because I went for two job interviews that week and I was offered both positions. The first was as an immigration officer based at Gatwick, and the second was with a small video production consultancy based in Didsbury, another suburb of Manchester. The Manchester job was less well paid than the Civil Service one, but in comparison to Income Support and a student grant before that it sounded like a fortune, and I accepted the offer immediately.

It seemed strange to pull on a smart pair of jeans and an ironed shirt at eight a.m. on Monday morning and take the bus to my new place of work. I thought of Ben as I had left him, sipping tea and sitting in his dressing-gown by the window.

I had known, really, even as I was experiencing it, that my unemployment had been a flirtation with nothingness. Like that first summer Ben and I spent sitting around, it had to come to an end, despite an insistent feeling of permanence at the time. Ben was working harder than ever, too, and I had just come to be a distraction for him, the way I crept around the flat attempting to read, and failing to be anything other than bored and annoying.

My duties were unclear at work. Though I have a good degree in English Lit., I was starting out as more or less a general dogsbody and tea maker. But at least the process of script work and consultancy were being shown and explained as they occurred around me. There was a small studio in the attic which was used occasionally for taped interviews and training films. They were not an in-house production unit, but had pretensions to becoming one once they could afford bigger premises.

I was given a stack of information to read up about video production, script work and the relevant technicals of lighting and electronics. But initially I was the one to hold the gaffer tape, to drive out to pick up materials, or to two finger type a revised script. The menial nature of what I was doing didn't alter the fact that I thought it was all fantastic. I dreamed constantly of greater and greater things and felt, at last, that something was happening to me that I could grasp and build on – something that wasn't just a whilst-I-can't-think-of-anything-better-to-do affair, like my decision, way back, to study English.

EIGHTEEN
TAG

The evening I went back with Ben and Malcolm I was feeling weak and in need of attention. I suggested going home with them partly because I wanted the company, and partly because I knew it was a possibility that I could get them both into bed and I wanted to exert some of my influence – just to prove that I could do it.

I now think that I turned all pathetic with Ben because I'd been feeling freaked-out by my encounter with Andy and had regarded Ben as someone with a kind of intrinsic understanding of what I was feeling; an assumption that was crazy because he's not the type of person who could ever understand the motivation behind violence (which is why he forgave me so easily for what I did to him in his kitchen).

When I got back to their place with them, I realised what a huge mistake it all was. Ben went kind of proprietorial, which made me want to puke. He made me lie down and went off to get some massage oil, and a blanket for me to lie on. I pretended to be more drunk than I was because I didn't want expressions of closeness. Then, I'd needed clean, emotionally untainted sex – which is what I'd had with Malcolm before, but which now seemed impossible with Ben around. He was bringing such a load of unrelated emotional garbage to the incident that it rendered it worthless to me – made it into some big event, when really it should only have been sex.

I have to admit that the massage was great. Just what I needed as it happens. I'd thought sex would be a good way of blowing off steam, but the massage did it for me much more effectively. I found myself drifting off in a more easy way than I had done for a long time, and when I crawled into bed with them, Malcolm and Ben – but especially Ben – were inconsequential. Sex was irrelevant. All I wanted was sleep.

When I woke up, it was five-thirty and I had the

beginnings of a hangover. I hadn't realised I'd drunk so much the previous evening. Ben and Malcolm were out cold so I slipped out of the bed and drank a glass of water, then dressed and left. It was already light outside, and still, and cool.

No, I'd thought, it wasn't worth it. I couldn't help shivering at the idea of waking up with them and having to put up with all the cuddling and hugging that seems to go on in the aftermath of sleeping with someone like Ben. Perhaps they would have wanted sex; but post-coital cosiness is something that strikes me as being fundamentally dishonest. When I've ejaculated I think to myself, *Right, let's get on with the day*. I hate this affirmation crap. I don't need to be cuddled and it makes me feel dissipated if I do it to others.

If only we'd gone back to my place rather than theirs, I'd have been able to control the situation; I wouldn't have allowed Ben to take over like that.

The following week, Malcolm phoned me on the Friday and invited me out to a restaurant to celebrate his first week of employment. I asked if Ben was going to be there and he said, `Of course,' in a kind of belligerent way as if to say that the ball was now in my court. I balked at that but said nothing, thinking privately that it would be pretty easy to burn Ben off somehow, once an opportunity arose.

Nevertheless, despite the aggression in Malcolm's tone, there was a flirtation too, a sexy come-on that may not have been deliberate, but it was definitely there and I interpreted it as a continuing fascination with me. I decided that – so long as I could be emphatically in control – maybe it *was* worth a charity fuck with Ben to get my hands into Malcolm's pants again.

I agreed to meet them at the restaurant and went along feeling brighter than I have for a long time. Ben and Malcolm were already there eyeing the menu. Ben leaned forward and touched my elbow as I sat down, a gesture of affection that I found particularly creepy and oddly threatening. He smiled in a conciliatory way and it made me want to mash his face into the pristine cotton tablecloth. Still, I handled myself well and at the end of the meal I suggested that they come back to my place for coffee rather than having it at the restaurant, and they agreed. I felt sure of myself that evening, which gave me a sense of power and control.

As we walked back to my place, everything was different. For a start, we were going to be on my territory, so I could kick them out whenever I wanted to. My bed is only just big enough for two to sleep in, so it would be impossible for three and that would make an easy excuse for asking them to leave.

I was looking forward to being in charge this time and, though this is kind of hard to admit, I was also beginning to be intrigued by Ben. I wanted to see what he was like in bed. How did he make love? That would be the most revealing thing of all. If I observed that, then I would have even more power, the most useful power of all – the ability to inflict emotional pain.

In the end, he turned out to be quite a surprise. I didn't expect him to be so physically assured and though he accepted a certain amount of horseplay, he had the ability to steer the situation clear of anything even remotely dangerous before it arose. I couldn't help respecting him for this even whilst it annoyed me that I didn't have more control over him. He actually pressed me back onto the bed at one stage with the palm of his hand, and though he did it without a great deal of pressure, for the first time in my life I found it impossible not to give in. I lay back and let him minister to me. Malcolm was more inhibited with Ben there, and I could see why. The kind of sex we'd had before would have been much too superficial for Ben. He seemed to be delving into some deep emotional space in both of us and I found myself responding by letting him in; a strangely painful experience that left me uncertain of our roles – a situation that I hadn't anticipated and which I disliked in spite of a certain relief at being able to give in to someone, just once, for a moment.

In the nude Ben actually had a certain unity that couldn't be called skinny because no part of him was too

75

thin for his frame. He was lean and had a steadiness about him that made him seem older and more experienced than he was. Maybe it was the fact that he knew what he wanted and didn't hesitate to go for it.

Malcolm, on the other hand, seemed freaked-out at the situation and waited to take all his cues from Ben, and thus didn't wrestle or laugh after our first tumble onto the bed. When I was lying there on my back, Ben and Malcolm attending to me, I couldn't help getting the impression that the two of them were making love to each other through me. I can't think of any other way to describe it. I felt marginalised into a mere duct for their feelings for each other. This was patently not the case, because Ben was extremely attentive. It must have been the fact that I had relinquished my hold on the situation that made me feel insignificant. Even when I came, I felt that nothing particular had happened, and the closeness of damp flesh within the restricted boundary of my bed was enough to make me retch. Ben, after he'd come, looked as if he'd exerted himself incredibly and lay with his leg crooked over my thigh. He leant over and smiled before kissing me. I kissed him back without thinking, then pushed his leg away and got out of bed quickly to go off and make us all some coffee. Leaving the room, I stood in the kitchen and thought, *What was that?*

NINETEEN
BEN

When you asked us back for coffee I knew we were going to make love. I was torn in the most painful way by the need to say yes and the need to say no. On one hand, I wanted to make love because I fancied you. On the other, I could see this terrible hardness in your eyes, this monumental will not to soften, and especially not to soften for me. I was aware of the aridness of your sexual past. No one who has ever experienced love could behave in the way that you did. I wanted to go home with you and – with Malcolm's help – show you what making love can be like.

Right, I thought to myself, *so long as you do this with care, you have the ability to bestow something important on someone who needs it.*

Malcolm had his own agenda and his own reasons for wanting this to happen and I wasn't naive enough to assume he'd ever tell me them. We had to go through this together, but separately, the three of us. How we had got into this situation was a good question, but I recognised that the way out of it was not to backtrack – it was to go on through whatever was on our horizon.

Maybe you felt this too and that was why you were so passive when we were in bed. I must say I was surprised because I expected you to use your physical strength as an intrinsic part of your love-making, to use it to stay in charge of what was going on, just as you had made it central to the outward expression of your sexuality.

When you lay back I could see that you were confused and that made me feel strong, because even though you were more than ten years older than me, and you'd seen the world, I had something that you'd never had – the ability to give, emotionally – and I could see that it scared you. It made you feel inferior, which was something that you'd spent your whole life trying to avoid.

Afterwards, when you dashed off like that following the briefest of kisses, I knew the scenario had been played out in a way that you hadn't anticipated. Malcolm and I lay together, slightly shy of each other after what we'd done. It had been like this in the sauna too, Malcolm lying there, surprised that I had been the one to take the initiative in the sexual encounter once it had been triggered. He smiled at me in an `I'm not sure what to say' sort of way. I smiled back and hugged him and felt absolutely in control and unthreatened.

`I think he needed that,' I whispered. `Some affection.'

Malcolm nodded and lay looking up. Then he got up and dressed and went out to talk to you. I got up too and dressed more slowly, thinking how stupid it is to have preconceptions about who people are. We all hide behind facades, and yours was just bigger and showier than most and hid a petrified child in need of love. Well, right at that moment, I felt I had some to spare.

I pulled on my black sweatshirt and turned to look at my hair in the mirror. The couple of weeks since I'd had it cut short had made all the difference and I looked very cool, I thought, and bright and young. I rubbed it so it was spiky and then went through to see you and Malcolm. You were whispering and looked as though you were angry – or at least disagreeing – about something. But I couldn't hear what you were saying and you turned and saw me and picked up a coffee and handed it to me, perfunctorily.

`Sorry I can't offer to let you stay,' you said. `It's not really practical.'

`That's okay,' I told you. `We'll go after coffee. It's late anyway,' and I thought how sad it was that you were already regretting what had happened.

78

TWENTY
MALCOLM

In bed, Tag was so different to how he'd been before. It was as if he was mesmerised by Ben. When we undressed, Tag virtually ignored Ben, making it clear that he was putting up with him only as a way of getting off with me. I found this both insulting to Ben and a huge ego boost to me. But when we got onto the bed and lay so close, he couldn't ignore Ben and became hesitant in his arms, and distant, which was a real surprise to me. So much so, in fact, that I became a mere observer, realising that something extremely complicated was going on behind Tag's closed eyes, but being utterly unable to guess what it was. Ben, however, seemed to have some kind of understanding that was almost telepathic and he treated Tag without the need for words, in a way that was verging on being eerie. I had never seen Ben like this, so completely in control – of both of us. There was something wild, too, about what was going on – not physically, because it was restrained to the point of inertia – but the atmosphere was palpable as a current between them. It made me feel excluded, though not unduly threatened because the current was one way only. It was going from Ben to Tag. Tag was not reciprocating in any way; he was just lying there and taking it. Later, Ben gave me more attention, but I was never really a part of it.

Tag's orgasm was so internalised that I had no idea that he had come until I was startled by the warmth of his semen against my skin. I had come a couple of minutes before and had become even more of a spectator, which was interesting in a slightly freaky way and made me realise how impossible it is to really know what is going on in another person's head.

Ben kissed him and then Tag leapt out of bed as though he'd woken from a nightmare and, grabbing his clothes, dashed off to the kitchen mumbling something about making us some coffee. Ben lay there looking incredibly

79

smug and happy. I looked at the clock by the bed and noticed that it was after midnight. I lay there without being able to think of anything to say and Ben rolled over and hugged me and I felt that this evening, somehow, he had a surfeit of love to give and I just reclined beside him and let it flow into me.

After a couple of minutes, I got up and followed Tag into the kitchen. He was bashing mugs about on the sideboard and sloshing water into the kettle, furious. I went up behind him and put my arms round his waist and he jumped with shock, tensing, twisting round as though he was going to hit me, and then going limp in my arms.

`Oh,' he said, `I thought you were Ben.'

`Calm down,' I said. `What's the matter?'

`I'm not doing that again,' he hissed. `No way. Ben's weird and I'm not going to screw around with him, not even for you. He's had his charity fuck and that's my side of the bargain seen to. Next time you come over, come on your own.'

`What's your problem?' I hissed back. `Don't pretend you didn't do this of your own free will. Don't make your anger out to be Ben's fault. It's crazy. Just calm down.'

Tag poured out the coffee and then turned and looked at me.

`I never want to see Ben again,' he said. `He makes me want to puke. He's so fucking gooey, being in bed with him is like eating too many sweets. I gave up that adolescent deep-and-meaningful crap before I was nineteen. It's a pile of shit.'

And there was Ben in the doorway, dressed and smart. Tag went over to him and thrust a coffee towards him.

`Sorry I can't offer to let you stay,' he mumbled. `It's not really practical.'

`That's okay,' Ben said. `We'll go after coffee. It's late anyway,' and he looked at me with a kind of pitiful resignation that made me realise that the strength I'd seen in him only a few minutes before had only been in the context of what he was doing then. Now, Tag was so far beyond him that they couldn't hope to reach each other.

And why should Ben want to try, I thought, considering their relationship to date?

When we left, I took Ben's elbow and he leaned in close to me as we walked home.

`This is ridiculous,' I said. `Tag's not that important. I don't really want to see him again.'

`Don't say anything now,' Ben said. `See how you feel later.'

But something definitive had changed in my attitude towards Tag. I now felt profoundly uncurious about him, which was odd seeing as previously I'd had what amounted to a fixation. I could see now, through the way that Ben had related to him, what a genuinely screwed-up individual he was. I realised that, actually, I had been attracted to Tag's stability rather than his body, and now that I had discovered him to be weak, I found I didn't really want to see him again, and I didn't think that time would make me change my mind – precisely the opposite, more likely. In time I would probably look back and wonder how ludicrous it was that I'd fallen for him in the first place.

TWENTY ONE
TAG

I had always known that my father was intensely unhappy. Life with my mother was as painful for him as it obviously was for her and I think he was only sticking around because of me – either that or he was the victim of some kind of deeply misogynistic masochism. By the time I was nine I was well aware of being regarded as a burden. Sometimes my father would come in from work, pissed out of his skull, and if my mother was away at one of her bridge afternoons, he'd lock me in one of the small outhouses where he stored fertilizer and rough, empty hessian sacks.

At first I hated the dark and the cramped conditions, and bashed on the door and shouted for help, but my father would beat me if I made a noise, and so I gave up. After a while I found I could burrow into the pile of sacks and curl up as if hibernating. This was fine in the summer, but when it was cold, the thick stone walls of the outhouse radiated a chill into my bones. In spite of my covering I would feel an agonizing discomfort that would gradually become a creeping numbness. I would lie there hoping that I'd be let out before too long. Usually I was only shut in for an hour or so. Dad would release me as soon as he heard my mother's car on the drive outside. I could make out the crunch of tyres on gravel through the door, and it was an immediate relief to hear it. I never told my mother about this treatment from my father because I knew he would find out and beat me for it – and when he lost his temper, his beatings were worth avoiding.

One day Tim, one of the farm hands, opened the outhouse door whilst I was locked in and yelled out when he saw me. My father rushed through from his workshop and belted him across the side of his head, then pulled me out into the yard where I collapsed because my legs had gone to sleep and I couldn't stand up. He dragged me to the side door, leaning back and slapping my legs and calling me a lazy bastard. He beat me that evening with his leather belt and locked me in my bedroom until breakfast the following day. I still remember Tim's frightened face as my father hit him. He was sacked soon after that.

One hot summer's afternoon I was locked in the outhouse and

I heard my mother arriving home. But no one came to open the door. Instead I could hear the distant sound of a mammoth row in progress – and then the sound of the front door slamming and a car driving off. After a while I bashed on the door, but I was so hot and cramped and uncomfortable that I fell into a kind of doze eventually. When I woke up I felt sick and dizzy, but I tried bashing some more to try and alert someone. Even a thrashing would be preferable to staying where I was. After ten minutes or so, my mother timidly opened the outhouse door and let me out. She hadn't heard the noise herself, but had been informed of it by one of my father's employees.

When I got out, I vomited on the cobbles and my mother hurried me off to the bathroom to clean me up. She didn't say a word to me. She just knelt in front of me and wiped my face and cried so hard the tears dripped from her chin.

TWENTY TWO

BEN

Of course, I couldn't get you out of my mind. I left it a couple of days and then, on the Monday, I had to go round to see you. Malcolm had gone off to work looking incredibly motivated and I'd wandered into to my study and stared at the computer screen for a couple of hours, doing virtually nothing.

By lunch time I knew that I was preoccupied by the need to see you, so I walked over without phoning first because I didn't want you to fob me off with some excuse as to why you couldn't see me.

When I got to your flat, the door was hanging askew, presumably shouldered off its hinges by some thug. I gingerly stepped into the small hallway and called your name, wondering if perhaps the perpetrators of this damage might still be around. I stood for a moment in the silence, poised to bolt if necessary. But there was no sound, so I heaved the door up and propped it in such a way that it would, hopefully, not look so inviting to burglars. Then I started to look around the flat to see if anything obvious had been stolen. There was no sign of theft, which made the quiet flat seem eerie. I peered cursorily into the bedroom, in passing, and saw that you were on the bed, naked, face down and apparently unconscious. The shock of seeing you so unexpectedly made me jump and catch my breath, and I steadied myself in the doorway before I could bring myself to approach you.

You were tied up, with thick bandages instead of rope, at wrists and ankles, attaching you to the head and foot of the bed. There were a series of bruises on your back and legs and a gash on your forehead that had bled substantially and had caused you to look almost deformed as you lay, swollen faced, on the blood-darkened pillow. Fortunately I didn't have to wonder whether you were dead because you were breathing with a quiet rasp.

I didn't know if I should move you or not and I stood for

a while, looking down at the bandages and feeling the stirrings of nausea at the sight of them, so painfully tight where they had bitten deep into your skin. I have always had a fear of bandages. They have symbolised death to me for as long as I can remember – right back to the dim shadow of my brother's drowning. But here, as I stood beside you, I realised that I had to overcome this irrational fear and get on with helping you.

I tried to untie the knots, which were drastically tight. I suppose you must have struggled with your bonds, constricting them further. Eventually I had to resort to a serrated cooking knife and hacked my way through them. After I got your wrists free, you groaned twice and opened your eyes.

`Hang on,' I said and started at your ankles.

When I'd released you, you turned slowly over onto your back and lifted your hand to your lips and felt in your mouth with your fingers.

`No teeth missing,' you whispered, `thank God.'

`Shall I call an ambulance?' I asked, thinking you looked really bad. But this panicked you and you said, `No! No! Please, just run me a bath. Luke warm.'

I did so and when I came back you were sitting up on the bed feeling round your rib cage for damage, looking dazed and grim.

`What happened?' I asked.

`Andy,' you said. `This guy you don't know, sent some heavies from London last night . . . '

I helped you off the bed and we staggered through to the bathroom. Once in the water, you looked less battered, somehow. Taking your flannel, I gently bathed your forehead, making you wince once or twice. But it wasn't as bad as it looked and, once I'd cleaned up the caked blood, it was clear that you'd been given a glancing blow by a shoe or boot that had scuffed you badly above your left eye, but no worse. You drank some water and then got out of the bath, pausing to look at yourself in the mirror. You stood there, inspecting your face, and then you turned to me and grinned.

`Shit,' you said. `That was quite a night. I'm starving.'

I cooked you bacon, eggs and fried bread and put on a jug of coffee.

`I knew it,' you said. `Even when I had my scene with Andy I knew he wasn't the kind of person to take a beating without retaliation. Julia, a mutual friend of ours, gave him my address in Manchester.'

And then you laughed, you actually laughed, and winced with the pain of it.

`He knows how to get his own back . . . '

After you'd eaten (you offered me some, but I had no appetite after dealing with all that blood) you stood up and put your arms round me and we went through to the front room.

`Thanks for coming round. I could have been there for days if you hadn't shown up. I owe you one,' and you kissed me on the lips. `I'd suggest we went to bed, but I'm not up to it right now.'

`That's okay. It's not why I came round. I just wanted to see you.'

You nodded and looked suddenly tired, half collapsing onto the settee. I sat beside you and you put your arm round my shoulder.

`All these terrible things I've done in my time . . .' you said. `I deserved this.'

`No one deserves what happened to you,' I replied, which made you laugh in a derisory way as though you thought I was saying something ridiculous.

`Sure,' you said, `sure. What do you know about it?'

I shrugged and you said, `I deserved it alright.'

There was a defiance in your voice as you said it, as though you expected me to argue. But I didn't know enough to have any point of reference; I didn't know what you had done to reap this degree of retaliation. I didn't ask for further details because I didn't want to know. I was already aware that there were these two sides to you – the hard side and the vulnerable side – and I didn't want to be exposed to the hard side any more than necessary. The vulnerable side seemed well hidden right now and you were blocking me every time I asked questions about how you felt and how hurt you thought you were. I reckoned you should go to a doctor, but you laughed at my suggestion and said you'd been through worse than this and still survived.

I remembered having made love to you a couple of days before. Whereas then you'd been all too willing to submit to me, now you were hard, in control of yourself, and perhaps a little embarrassed that I was here to remind you of the fact that you had relinquished yourself to me. Embarrassed, though grateful because I had rescued you.

When I got up to leave, you tried to look nonchalant, but there was something yearning in your eyes as though you wanted me to take over again, to coset you and look after you. But you said, `Thanks for coming round. See you, then,' and I let myself out after you'd kissed me briefly in an absent-minded way.

`Come round soon,' you said, `and don't forget, I owe you one. I always pay my debts.'

It was an odd way of saying it, but I took it as I assumed it was meant. You were saying that you were offering to make love to me again, but terms like `making love' were far too personal for you. `I owe you one' was about as close as you could get, and it intrigued me still that you were so far from making the connection between your impersonal exterior and your internal needs. Still, perhaps in time I could help to break down that barrier.

As I walked home, I realised that I had seen your duality as a challenge – a personal challenge to dig away all the garbage that was cluttering your life, and make you accept the part of you that you'd already shown me with such shame and regret.

TWENTY THREE
MALCOLM

Of course I felt like a hypocrite, but I hated the fact that Ben would go to see Tag without me. I'd decided, for myself, that I didn't want to see him again, so I wasn't jealous of the time Ben might spend with him – I was just jealous of any other person, whoever they were, being with Ben, and especially of the idea of them going to bed together. Tag had told me he didn't want to have sex with Ben again, but I knew that he was strangely powerless in Ben's presence, and it seemed inevitable that they would have sex at some point whilst I was at work. The mere thought of this made me seethe in a frightening way.

When Ben told me that Tag had been beaten up, it didn't surprise me. I think I'd come to know Tag well enough to realise that he was a wide-boy with dangerous acquaintances. It crystallised my dislike of him and I encouraged Ben to drop him, but he seemed caught up in some idea of having a great mission to rehabilitate Tag – a mission destined to failure, I reckoned, but such a sentiment would only have sounded like hypocrisy coming from me, so I kept quiet.

My big worry was the anger that I knew Tag held against Ben. From previous conversations I realised that Tag was capable of really going for him if pushed too far into an emotional corner – and now that Tag turned out to be more deeply involved with violence than I thought, it was awful to speculate how much further he might go than simply bashing Ben's head against a wall.

I couldn't talk to Ben about this because, by referring to these conversations with Tag, I would be admitting to a dirty subterfuge which would reflect badly on me. So I decided to leave things as they were. I would discourage this continuing friendship with Tag without actually forbidding it – which I had no right to do.

Tag phoned the evening after he'd been rescued by Ben and asked me if I wanted to go round at some point, but I said no.

`Why?'

`This friendship is over,' I told him. `I've realised that you're not the person I thought you might be. There's no point discussing it. I don't want to see you again.'

Tag laughed at this, which frightened me even more and made me wonder if he was capable of using Ben by way of retaliation. I desperately wanted to warn Ben, but my fears sounded pathetic if I said them aloud, and so I said nothing.

TWENTY FOUR
TAG

It's just as well I didn't decide to buy a place in Manchester. It turned out to not to be such a great place after all, which was a disappointment to me after its original promise. London seems to be a bit of a no-no for me now. Edinburgh has kind of bad associations, and I've always disliked Bristol, so I've been thinking of moving back to Yorkshire. Yorkshire has definite possibilities.

I made a few enquiries about places to stay and found that a couple of my old friends are still around – just outside Bradford – and prepared to put me up for a while. I feel good about moving on again. My Manchester experiment was a disaster, like so many other places I've tried, but that's okay. Malcolm turned out to be a huge disappointment. He was a wimp too, despite my initial impression of him, and I hung around all that time for nothing.

I gave my landlord a month's notice, so I have a timeframe for my departure, which makes me feel suddenly unpressurised and free. A couple of days after giving my notice, Ben came round. At first I wondered if I should just tell him to piss off, but then I decided to ask him in. It was too good an opportunity to waste.

`You're looking better,' he said and moved to kiss me, but I pushed him away.

`No,' I said. `No kissing. That's all over with. I'm splitting. I'm leaving Manchester and going back to Yorkshire.'

`Why does that mean you can't kiss me?'

`Because I don't want to kiss you. I never have.'

`Then why did you ever do it?'

`For Malcolm.'

I nodded him into the sitting room and he sat on the settee looking confused.

`You're a wimp,' I told him. `I've always despised you, and now that I'm going I might as well be honest about it. You're pathetically blighted by your past. So much so that you've never even learned how to live in the present. A tough past should give a person strength for the present – that's what it did for me. But it's given you nothing but a whole barrage of tedious complexes and insecurities.'

`If that's the way you feel, why have you ever had anything to do with me?'

`Because I wanted Malcolm. He made it clear that if I wanted to get into bed with him, then I had to be nice to you. It was hard work, but I managed it for a while. I even agreed that I'd give you a charity fuck if it made him more available. He was pretty good in bed, too, or at least he showed promise, so I reckoned it was worth it. But now he's fucked off, so I guess that's it. Now that he's gone, there's hardly any point being polite to you, is there?'

Ben looked at me with a slack jaw and I laughed inwardly.

`You don't attract me physically,' I went on. `I wouldn't have been able to get a hard-on if Malcolm hadn't been there. I'm sorry, but it's true. You might as well know.'

He nodded to himself as I said this, as though it was all slotting into place.

`The best thing you can do for Malcolm is let him go. You're dragging him into your own particular brand of nothingness. You know this, don't you? You've leeched all the life out of him and given him nothing in return but utter blandness. You've ruined your own life well enough, it seems sad that you're ruining his. You stopped him having what might have been something kind of exceptional with me. How many other opportunities have you made him miss?'

He sat there with a face that was blank. I tried not to smile.

TWENTY FIVE
BEN

When my mother got married for the second time, Uncle Gordon didn't come to the wedding. It caused raised eyebrows amongst the rest of the family, but I saw his point. One Sunday a few weeks later, when I was round at another aunt and uncle's place, Uncle Gordon turned up and got the frosty treatment. My stepfather wasn't there, so Gordon spoke his mind. 'How could you?' he asked my mother. 'How could you go from one bastard to another?' and she cried, and Aunt Pat said, 'How could you talk to her like that? Your own sister.' And he said, 'I can talk like that BECAUSE she's my sister. No one else has got the nerve to tell her the truth.'

'Well,' said Aunt Pat, 'that's rich seeing the mess you made of your marriage.'

'I'm not denying that I made a mess of things. That's precisely why I'm in a position to pass an opinion.'

The following week he was in a car accident and broke both his legs, and Aunt Pat said, 'Serves him right.'

We saw a lot less of Gordon after that, but it didn't stop him offering me a job on the local paper when I graduated. When I decided to stay in Manchester with Malcolm after university and there was that awful rumpus about it, he sent me a note which read: 'You're best out of it, Ben. Nothing good ever happened to this family. Stay away from it.'

* * * * *

I walked home from Tag's feeling empty and remembering that note. Perhaps it was something genetic in me – something in our family that caused us all to fail in our relationships. Maybe Tag was right and I should let Malcolm go. He seemed so much happier now that he was working and seeing less of me. Maybe I *was* holding him back?

I got home and managed a couple of hours typing before Malcolm came home. He noticed I was subdued but I told him it was because of the drudgery of my typing and I

92

think he believed me. We ate quite late and, because it was the student rave night, he suggested that we went down to Cruz.

Okay, I thought, *I may as well.*

I fancied getting drunk, though I knew it would probably make me feel worse. But sometimes you just have to wallow. It's the only way to work your way through a bad situation. And I did feel bad, and I couldn't talk to Malcolm about it because I didn't know how true the things were that Tag had told me – about Malcolm insisting on Tag being pleasant to me as a price for his favours.

I felt a certain relief in the knowledge that neither of us would ever see Tag again. Maybe I just had to face a few home truths about myself and take it from there, with Malcolm or maybe even without him.

Cruz was packed as usual with the student crowd. There was a time when I would have known a dozen or more people down here as soon as I walked through the door, but tonight I knew no one. That is the nature of student life, I guess, but it made me feel alien – as though I'd outstayed my welcome. Malcolm seemed oblivious to my mood. He'd had a talk with his boss that day who had told him that his prospects were extremely good, so I'm not surprised that he wasn't able to see my distress. I didn't want to spoil his mood, anyway, and ended up trying to appear cheerful for his sake.

I enjoy dancing. There is something incredibly hypnotic about letting yourself go on the dance floor. It was as if all the negative feelings that were stored up in me about Tag came out, then, although it didn't leave me happy. It left me feeling hollow. I realised that I had wanted to make love to him on my own, without Malcolm there. I had wanted to overpower him with my affection and force him to open up to me. But that was ridiculous, I now realised. I was lucky not to have got more physically hurt – though his verbal attack on me was devastating and presumably premeditated.

I found that I was dancing round by the side of the speaker system, as though trying to hide. Malcolm and I had become separated by the crowd and he was further out on the dance floor. In the wake of Tag's attack on me, I felt somehow negated, physically. He'd certainly known how to hit where it hurt, especially seeing as I'd thought he'd started to fall for me. But maybe I wasn't good-looking. Perhaps he was right in saying that I spent my time trailing in the wake of Malcolm's attractiveness.

I ended up standing near the bar drinking Red Stripe with Malcolm, watching the crowd. There was a cute guy over to my left who was watching us. I smiled at him and he smiled back and I felt a desperate need for physical affirmation right now, which was followed by a surge of anger that I should even consider that reassurance was important. It made me feel that I was trivialising everything by placing it on a material level. What did it matter what I looked like? If Malcolm wanted me, then that should be enough.

Malcolm went off to the toilet and I glanced over at the guy, a man in his mid-twenties, perhaps, who was tall and assured. He sauntered over to me and leant close to my ear to make himself heard.

`Was that your boyfriend?' he shouted.

`Why?' I shouted back.

`He's horny. I've been watching him all evening.'

`Yes,' I told him. `We're together.'

`Pity.' The man shrugged and wandered off leaving me feeling suddenly blown apart, emotionally dismembered, with Tag's accusations running through my mind; and even though I knew he had vindictively said them in the hope that this would happen – I couldn't stop them. I felt tawdry, dull, bereft of any redeeming qualities. I was just a drunk typist who had had absurd ambitions of becoming someone of real merit. And I had failed utterly to be anything I had ever set out to become. Like my mother. Like Uncle Gordon. Like my father. Like everyone in my sordid family.

`Come on,' I said to Malcolm when he came back, `I've had enough. I'm tired.'

We walked to the taxi rank in silence and Malcolm

94

draped his arm over my shoulder and kissed me. I think I managed a smile, and when we went to bed, Malcolm fell asleep almost immediately, leaving me alone in the darkness of our room.

I got up again at around three and slipped out of the flat, making my way over to Richard's place. I knew it was foolish to disturb him at this hour, but I was beginning to feel irrational and had to anchor myself somehow. Of course, I should have woken Malcolm and talked to him then, but he seemed so inert and distant that I couldn't do it.

When Richard opened the door, he looked both concerned and pissed off, and ushered me inside.

`What's wrong?' he asked me.

`I don't know,' I told him.

He made me sit down and then sat opposite me on a wooden chair and took my hands in his.

`Look,' he said, `it's got to be something.'

`I think I want to sleep with you,' I said.

`What, now?'

`Yes, I think so.'

`Ben, you don't come out with propositions like that at three-thirty in the morning. You're being absurd. And anyway, what about Malcolm?'

It was a valid question and one I had no answer to. We sat in silence, me gazing at the floor for some time before looking up into Richard's eyes. Richard leaned closer and pulled my head forward so it was resting on his shoulder.

`Is it something to do with Tag?' he asked.

I shrugged and he sighed and ran his fingers through my hair.

`Please,' I said, `let me spend the night with you.'

`No, Ben, you'd only regret it. Come back tomorrow and we'll talk about it. I finish at four so you can come over then. You can sleep in the spare bed if you don't want to go home.'

`No,' I sighed. `I'll go. Thanks anyway.'

We sat on for a while, not speaking, but Richard was nodding off, so I got up to leave. He hugged me on the doorstep, struggling to stay awake, and asked if I was sure

I didn't want to sleep in the spare room. I said I'd be okay and left feeling ridiculous and wondering what I had expected to happen. Physical reassurance, perhaps, but the timing was crazy, and I would only have been using Richard in a selfish way, for reasons that had nothing to do with our friendship. When things fall away inside, it seems, there is no external help to be found to put them back in place.

EPILOGUE

MALCOLM

I'm sitting here, clearing out one of Ben's drawers, trying to find a clue as to why he might have left. In the drawer there is a box of drawing pins; a pen knife; a postcard to him from me with a blue vase on the front and addressed to *Ben Vard (the loveliest person in the world)*; a note from Richard thanking him for a pleasant evening; a copy of James Kirkup's poem: *The Love That Dares to Speak Its Name*; an expired one year passport; a bulldog clip; a couple of pebbles from the beach; a small photo album with pictures of him as a child; two loose paracetamol tablets; a safety pin; an unidentifiable Yale key; a broken scalpel; the note of apology from Tag, and a photo booth strip of the two of us horsing around, kissing and laughing.

But there's nothing to give me a definite clue. I can only assume it was because of Tag and the way I dragged him into our set-up with such selfish abandon. There is a link, or a reason, though I don't suppose it will ever become clear. It amazes me now that I thought of Ben and Tag as being so disparate, when in fact they had a fundamental similarity: an outward appearance of stability founded on a need to hide its opposite. Whether this realisation is in any way constructive to me now, I don't know. I hope so, because what other good can I salvage from what we all went through?

ADDY, LAURA &
OLD JACK BUTLER

ONE

I heard the jangle of Addy's keys as she let herself into the house.

'Come on Paul,' she urged as she came into the front room, 'we're late.'

'Late for what?'

'Late for Old Jack Butler's funeral.'

'Who's Old Jack Butler?'

Addy clicked her tongue in disapproval.

'Doesn't your mum ever tell you anything?'

''Course not. Never does, never did, never will. Who was he?'

'He was someone important to us both, your mother and me.'

'Is mum coming to the funeral, then?'

'No, absolutely not. I only found out about it at the last minute.'

Addy was my best friend. My best, best friend. She always used to say that no seventeen-year-old should have best friends nearly twenty years older than themselves, but that was dumb, and besides, I knew she was pleased that I liked her so much. When I told her, recently, that she was my best friend, she said, 'What about Ian?' and I replied, 'Ian's my lover. That's different.'

'Isn't he your best friend as well as your lover?'

I thought about that for a moment, and replied, 'I don't know.'

'Well,' Addy had sighed, 'I don't like the sound of that.'

She'd looked down and then smiled at me.

'But you are young at least,' she'd added, as though that explained everything.

For as long as I could remember, Adeline had always taken me out on Saturdays so that mum could go off for the day and not worry about me. This arrangement went on long after I was old enough to look after myself – and long after Duncan had taken his place in my mother's bed. Duncan was thankful for anything and anyone that took me out of his way, and so he was grateful to Addy, though he resented her, too; they both did, my mum and Duncan. They resented her and were hostile towards her – hostile and yet needful.

Addy would take me away. She hated where I lived – an

101

intolerant, narrow-minded part of town, she called it. She'd drive me out into the countryside or to other towns where we'd walk in parks, go to the cinema, or to cafés where they put paper doilies under the cups. But it wasn't what we did that mattered – sometimes we did nothing more than laze around in her flat, drinking coffee and watching television. No, what mattered was our conversation. She talked to me. I mean, TALKED to me. She listened to all my dreams and sometimes she told me ones of her own.

Today, Addy looked dreamier than I'd ever seen her, in her black skirt and blouse, and her dark wool jacket with corded piping. She was holding in her hand a round pillbox hat with a veil that I knew would make her look fabulous. She dabbed at her slightly craggy eyes with a Kleenex and plumped her freshly permed hair. She opened her bag and took out a small envelope addressed to my mother and dropped it on the table – something she did every week – to let mum know that she was okay.

`Did you like this Jack Butler, then?' I asked as I tied the tie I hadn't worn in months.

`Did I like him? Did I like him! I loved him, that's what.' She dabbed again. `But it's too late to cry. Far, far too late.'

I'd never seen Adeline cry before. It suited her, softened her, made her look tragic, like a film star.

`Never regret the past,' I told her. `You've been telling me that for years. See to the present and the past will take care of itself.'

`But love turns all your best sayings upside down,' Addy sniffed.

She rang for a taxi in the kitchen.

`I expect they'll have champagne at the wake,' she said. `It's better if I don't drive.'

She became brisk as we waited, smoothing my hair with her hand, readjusting my tie. Usually she showed no interest in how smart I looked, so I knew that today she had a real sense of occasion.

✱ ✱ ✱ ✱ ✱

Let me tell you who I am – or at least how I see myself at the moment. These things change all the time, like the shifting clouds in the sky. By the time I've told you, I'll be different.

My name is Paul. My last name is irrelevant. I wouldn't like to tell you anything that might connect me too closely in your minds with my undeserving family. But perhaps you already know them, so what's the point in keeping quiet? If I'm going to tell this story, you might as well know everything.

My name is Paul Sandford. I live in the most parochial town in the universe. You've probably seen my mother down at Kwik Save. She's the one who always buys loaves of thick sliced family white bread for the freezer. She's the one who looks as though she's in slow motion. She's the one who looks as if life's treated her like shit (it has). You might have seen her with her man, Duncan, looking frazzled. He hates going into town with her, but mum can't drive and so he has to take her when she does her big shopping. He hovers around, not looking at anything, whilst my mother rummages through the bargain bin. I understand exactly why Duncan hates shopping with my mother; I hate it too. My mother's shopping habits imply that – due to Duncan's drinking and the fact that I am still at school – we would be firmly entrenched in poverty if it weren't for her careful budgeting.

My mother has sharp delineations – sharp shoulders, sharp hips and a sharp tongue. She is extravagantly thin and fragile-looking and appears to be too frail for the heavy stolidity of Duncan, whose hands alone look strong enough to extinguish her with ease. They both have tempers that get the neighbours whispering. Duncan's been with mum for five years and it feels like he's been around forever. He often shouts at me when he's had enough of shouting at the news, or about work, or at mum – or when he's had too much beer. His shouts are a reflex action when words fail him, which they do, often. He sometimes hits me to illustrate a point, but never hard enough for me to try and hit him back.

I'm doing my A levels. English, History and Geography. A provision for the future my mother says. A waste of fucking time, Duncan calls it. He could get me a job tomorrow working with him down at Coombes Yard. Of course, that's why I stayed on at school – precisely so that I would *never* have to work down at Coombes Yard. Ian's father works at Coombes too, though Duncan and Mr Levenson are a zillion miles apart on the ladder to senior management – I mean, Duncan is at the bottom and Mr Levenson is at least three quarters of the way to the top. They don't know that Ian and I know each other. We're careful to keep our relationship a big secret – big being the operative word. Duncan would blow his nut if he knew Ian and I were lovers. I think mum might be more understanding, but she's so frightened of anything that could be seen as a disadvantage in life, that she wouldn't be able to see the beauty in it for me.

Mum is frequently around during the day, so I can't really bring Ian round here. His parents both work, so we spend some of our time there. But, more than anything else, we go round to Addy's place, where she makes a fuss of us.

There is a reason why mum is often home. She has this inertia, like treacle in her veins. It's as if life sometimes becomes such a huge burden to her that she can barely move; can hardly get out of bed, and certainly can't make it to work. Eventually, absenteeism costs her her job. Oh, I've seen it. I've seen it so many times. I always dreaded the sight of her staggering to the top of the stairs in her dressing gown when she should have been at work. She would look down at where I stood gathering my books and she would say, `I can't make it Paul, I just can't. Would you mind phoning Mr Lockhart for me . . . '

Mr Lockhart, Mr Ashton, Mrs Dalziel, Ms Cole, Mr Frazer, Lena Farraday from Barts, Teddy Turner the butcher down the road who employed mum part-time and who came up the road in his bloodstained apron to sack her on our doorstep. (He'd been a friend before that.) I tell you, it wasn't easy, living with my mum.

When I was twelve, Duncan moved in, with his ex-army attitude and his anger and his desperate love for my mother – and this dislike of me that was so strong and so

104

confusing for him. He never guessed, later on, that I was gay; probably wouldn't have had it in him to even think along those lines. But he knew that I was different. He knew that I would never follow him to Coombes Yard, and he hated me for the criticism that he thought this implied. The mere fact that I might end up going to university seemed to make him feel that I reckoned he was shit (which I did, of course, but not for that reason).

He would sometimes come in at the end of the afternoon, on the rare occasions that mum would also be out at work and not back yet, and he would sneer at my homework spread out on the kitchen table. Sometimes he would hit me, especially if he'd had a couple of pints; or else he would send my books crashing to the floor with a sweep of his hefty arm. I would sit and look down at the papers, then slowly up at him and see that naked hurt in his face and the shattered past in his eyes, and I would hate him for taking it out on me; hate him for the fact that he would spread blame around him like stinking debris, spread it everywhere except the place where it belonged – with himself. I would hate him and gather up my work and take it upstairs to my sliver of a bedroom, where I would array it on my bed (there wasn't room in there for a desk).

`Let him die,' I would whisper, revelling in the intensity of my longing for him to be gone – a desire in which I could have absolute conviction because I knew that it wouldn't be fulfilled.

* * * * *

I remember I went out with Addy on my twelfth birthday. It was just before Duncan appeared on the scene, and after my mother had refused to be in the house when Addy came to collect me. Addy always arrived at mid-day, exactly. Mum left at quarter to. This was something that didn't make sense to me, but then so much of my life was incomprehensible that I didn't feel inclined, at the time, to wonder particularly about this.

That day, Addy took me out for an expensive lunch at a

restaurant in an old mill in the middle of nowhere that mum wouldn't dare to even dream of going to. (Not that she couldn't afford it, just once, if she'd really set her mind to it, but because it would have seemed to her such an absurd waste of money.) The meal was Addy's present to me because she had been forbidden, by my mother, from buying me presents.

'I can't buy you an object that you might take home with you,' Addy told me, 'so this will have to do instead. You mustn't tell Laura.'

I nodded my complicity, my mouth too full to speak.

When we were lingering over coffee, I said, 'How can you afford this, Addy?'

'I live on my own,' she replied. 'I have nothing and no one to spend my money on, except you.'

'About not telling mum . . . ' I said. 'You told me never to lie.'

'Ah,' Addy sighed. 'I did, didn't I? Well, there are at least two kinds of lying, you know: first, there's lying for the sake of yourself, for personal gain or to get out of your responsibilities; and secondly, there's lying in order to spare others hurt. The first kind of lying is bad; the second kind of lying isn't exactly good, but it isn't bad either. It's neutral.'

'Why would it hurt mum to know that you brought me here for lunch?'

'Just take it from me – she'd be hurt. Some things have no rational explanation. They just are.'

'Why is mum so unhappy?'

'Is she?' Addy looked at me across the starched table cloth and I could see a moistness in her eyes. 'Well, yes, I suppose she is.'

'How did that happen, then?'

'For a twelve-year-old you ask the most complicated questions,' Addy told me. She looked down into her coffee and I could see that she was trying to remember mum as she was once, ages ago.

'Laura was quite a rebel,' she told me. 'Not too bright at school, which didn't go down well with her father, who was a school teacher. Christine, your mother's elder sister, did well in her exams, but Laura . . . and it's not even as if these things are all that important in the end. The most important thing is to be able to do what you want – to be able to grab happiness when it fleets past you. To have the eyes to see it when it appears, and the wherewithal to seize it when it smiles at you.'

The waiter came by and poured us more coffee and leaned over Addy in a way that I thought strange, and he looked at her as if he thought she was the most beautiful person he had ever seen. I looked away and dug my teaspoon into the soft mound of brown sugar in the white china sugar bowl.

`Where was I?' Addy whispered to herself with a smile as the waiter wandered off. `Oh yes, Laura.'

She took out a small dispenser and popped two sweeteners into her cup, then smiled at me.

`Laura couldn't do it, you see, she couldn't live up to Christine. She was always trailing in her wake as far as her father was concerned. After a while she just didn't bother to go to school at all, which caused endless trouble. I didn't know her at that time, but I heard about it all later, from Christine and your grandfather. They talked to me about Laura as if she were a lost cause, even when she was there, in the room. It made me want to hit them. To tell the truth, it made me hate them.'

I can't imagine you hating anyone,' I said.

`Go on thinking of it as unimaginable,' she said, `because then, maybe, with luck, it'll never happen to you. Perhaps you'll be lucky enough to get through life without ever having the terrible experience of hating someone.'

❋ ❋ ❋ ❋ ❋

Aunt Christine came to dinner at about the time I told Addy she was my best friend. She came with Uncle Jez and Samantha, my cousin, and a friend of Samantha's – Becky. Everyone called her Becky except Aunt Christine who insisted on calling her Rebecca. She was thin and mannered and looked as though she was trying to balance a tiara on her well-groomed head. She had seen me, so Samantha whispered, in Burger King and had asked to be introduced. So here she was. `Why don't you ask her out for a date?' Sam whispered. I kept my face straight and expressionless for a few seconds, then I thought of Ian and had to look away and smile. I hadn't known Ian long at that time – maybe three months – and thinking of him still brought a smile to my lips. I couldn't help it. It just appeared on my face.

Samantha looked at me as though she was challenging me to prove something. What? That I was straight? Well, she could wonder all she wanted. I wasn't going to tell anyone one way or another, or at least not now. Once I'd got my A levels and a job, or a place at university, and left home, then, *then*, I'd take the greatest pleasure in making sure that everyone knew, in no uncertain terms, what it is that I prefer to do in bed. But now, I had Duncan to contend with, and Duncan could shout at me because I'd set the table badly, or because I was using up too much space to do my homework, or because he'd had a bad day at work. The less I told him about my life, the less he would be able to shout at me about it – especially if it had anything to do with boys loving boys.

`So,' Aunt Christine asked, looking at me, but talking to mum, `has Paul got a girlfriend yet?'

`Not as far as I know.'

`He's nearly Seventeen, Laura,' Christine told her.

`He's not normal,' Samantha asserted.

`Paul's got better things to do than date girls. There's nothing wrong with studying,' Laura huffed, `is there Duncan?'

Duncan looked at me with withering disdain and then agreed with Laura. He always agreed with Laura in front of Christine, whose caravan they were hoping to borrow for three weeks in the summer. *He* saw me as being not normal, but he could only see the world through his own eyes, which was lucky for me because, if he'd been able to see through mine, he'd see how much I hated him. Mum

108

was blind, too, but in her case it was wilful. I looked round the room and thought: *you're all blind*.

Christine came over to me and took my chin in her hand.

`Don't look so sour,' she smiled. `It spoils your face. I'm only teasing, Paul. It's just that you shouldn't see life as such a burden. You should get out and have some fun, a good-looking boy like you. I mean, by the time Laura was your age, she'd already had you . . . '

`But I never wanted to do A levels,' said Laura.

`No, no of course,' Christine agreed. `But that's not the point.'

`What is the point, Aunt Christine?' I asked her.

`Don't use that tone with me,' she said. `I'm not your enemy.'

`What tone do you mean?'

`There, you used it again. Polite but disdainful.'

`He needs a good thrashing,' said Duncan. `He uses it with me all the time.'

`You should get out of the house more often,' Christine told me. `You should be dating someone nice, like Rebecca.'

Becky smiled across and I suddenly wanted to slap her hard across her prim cheek, not because I wished her harm, but because I wanted to make it clear that this kind of interference was not welcome.

`I'm fine as I am,' I told my aunt and she laughed and said, `That's what you think.'

`Come on,' Sam said to me. `Come on into the kitchen and we'll make everyone some coffee.'

I followed her, Becky behind me. As soon as we were through the door, Sam flung her arms round my neck.

`Tell me,' she said, with her usual, insincere smile, `is it true?'

`What?'

`You know.'

`Do I?'

`Of course.'

`What?'

`Is it true that you're into boys?'

`What do you think?'
`I think that you are.'
`Then why ask?'
`Because I might be wrong.'
`And I might be a liar.'
`We're all liars,' she smiled.
She filled the kettle, then plugged it in.
`Right,' she said, smirking to Becky, `I'm off to the toilet.'
In the silence after her departure I could hear Becky breathing quickly.
`Why did Sam ask you that?' she said.
`You know Sam.'
`I'm not sure that I do, particularly.'
I began to assemble mugs. Becky leaned against the chipped white enamel of the sink and watched me. Her long, mid-brown hair was absolutely straight and she pushed it behind her ear with a peremptory flick of her fingers, then smiled at her feet. I could see, peripherally, her straight nose, and the fact that she was looking at me. She may have been attractive, but I chose not to think in those terms. She was there; I didn't want her to be there, and I resented her presence. What she looked like didn't concern me.
When Sam came back, she laughed.
`Did you ask him?'
`Shh,' said Becky.
I poured water over the instant coffee granules and added milk.
`Becky wants to ask you something.'
I put the mugs on the tray and, picking it up, walked to the door.
`Please,' said Becky, quietly.
I paused in the doorway.
`Please,' she said, `will you come and see me sometime?'
`Maybe,' I said, and left the room.

✳ ✳ ✳ ✳ ✳

Let me tell you how I first met and slept with Ian. It was

about nine months ago, now. I was in the pub one Friday night, celebrating the eighteenth birthday of Mel, a girl in my class. We were going on to a party afterwards and I'd arranged to stay over at the house of Pug, a boy from my class whose real name was Darren.

`I've invited Ian along,' Mel whispered, as though I should know who he was. `He's *amazing*, I mean, truly. All the girls fancy him, but especially me. God, his *eyes*! He's moved in down the road from us and he's absolutely . . . ' She sighed and gave up, lost for words, and sipped her sweet Martini and lemonade, complete with a maraschino cherry on a cocktail stick. She stirred the drink with her cherry before devouring it voluptuously.

`I love him,' she said with what amounted to either genuine sincerity (of which I doubted she was capable), or a monumental self-delusion that I rather despised her for. Still, it gave the evening a certain air of expectancy. I had an impression of what he would look like – tall and dark, and broad-but-elegant; secretive and fluid in his movements. I could visualise his expressive hands and their languid, careless gestures. I looked out for him all evening, and when he walked through the door, I recognised him immediately.

Mel gave a kind of excited moue, then a stifled shriek, and lunged across the bar to grab his arm.

`Ian!' she cried, `come and meet my friends.'

She introduced us in turn, but Ian looked only at me, or so it seemed, and I could tell this flustered Mel because she mumbled my name in passing and pulled him to the far side of the bar where I couldn't see him. But he had given me a conspiratorial smile, so I was unconcerned that I couldn't see him – I knew that our separation was only temporary.

By moving my chair back a little and joining in a bland conversation with Pug, I could see Ian's back and shoulder where he was sitting with Mel. He would turn slightly, every now and then, and glance across at me and smile. He was about my age, with a slightly flattened nose and deeply recessed eyes, but the line of his jaw was ardent and I could see the muscles playing under the skin as he clamped his teeth rhythmically to some internal cadence. Mel looked too, once, and frowned when she saw me and leaned in to talk even more loudly to Ian, as though she could seduce him by the mere force of her frenetic personality.

He had a line to his shoulders that made him look expectant, or hesitant, as though waiting – like an athlete in his blocks – for some phantom starting pistol to herald his escape. He looked as though he was being restrained, by his politeness and by his slow expansive movements, from leaving to join some unimaginably glamorous party from which he had become unaccountably detached.

When we went on to our own decidedly unglamorous party, we all stopped at an off-licence and bought some beers. Ian smiled and said, `Are you going to this party?' and I said, `Yes.' `I'll come too, then,' he said.

Mel came over and put her arm through his.

`Come outside,' she said. `I want you to meet someone.'

Ian shrugged at me, and smiled again – a smile that acknowledged a connection between us – and allowed himself to be towed out of the shop.

The party, when we got there, was loud and young and giddy and Mel boastingly introduced Ian to the other girls from school, clutching at him for as long as it took her to pass out on the sofa. Then, he came and joined me in the hall where two skinheads were collapsed together and three people were waiting in a queue for the toilet. He smiled at me, and I smiled back.

`I like your smile,' he said.

I was embarrassed by this comment, which made me smile even more. He clutched at his heart, theatrically, and flung himself back against the wall.

`Pierced!' he sighed. `My heart is pierced,' and he slid down the wall and lay at my feet.

`She doesn't like you,' he said, opening his eyes and looking up at me from the floor.

`Mel? No.'

`I think she fancies you too, or did.'

He got to his knees and wrapped his arms round my

thighs, using my body as a support up which he could clamber. When he was standing, we were nose to nose and I suddenly knew what Mel had meant when she'd sighed about his eyes.

`I suppose there was no joy to be had there, as far as her fancying you went?'

`No,' I said. `No joy.'

`I thought so,' he said. `Have you ever slept with a man?'

`Not as in spend-the-night-in-a-bed-with.'

`But you have done it?'

`Yes,' I said, `I've done it.'

`Do you want to do it again?'

We went up to the little spare room and we made love amongst the coats. He was supple and seemed to yield beneath my fingers in a certain plastic way, as though he was made of clay and the impression of my hands would remain sunk into his flesh forever. He was also restrained and a little clinical, I thought, but then we were immersed in coats, with the prospect of imminent discovery. He shied away from my penis in a way that made me feel strange, though it was our first time and I'd had no particular expectations.

Afterwards, he leaned towards me and whispered, `Why don't you come back tonight and sleep with me, as in *spend-the-night-in-a-bed-with*?'

`Is that okay?'

He nodded, so I nodded back and we left the party together without a word.

`My parents are at home, so we'll have to creep in, but they're off early tomorrow for the day, so if we lie low we'll be alright.'

I felt clandestine and adult, creeping up the stairs to Ian's bedroom. We kissed briefly and then he undressed quickly and pulled back the covers so that I could get into bed first. Once I was beside him, he put his arms round my chest from behind and fell asleep almost at once. I lay there listening to his breathing and to the night noises from outside, and I thought about how brief our sexual assigna-

113

tion amongst the coats had been, and how inevitable, given the quality of his first glance at me. I heard the house creaking as it cooled down, and I wondered how likely it was that I would be discovered in Ian's bed – and whether it would matter if I was.

In the morning I was startled awake by a knocking on the door. Ian leaned over me and put a finger to his lips and smiled.

`Yeah,' he called.

`We're off now,' came his mother's voice.

`Okay,' he called back. `See you later.'

`Around six.'

`Okay.'

`Bye.'

`Bye.'

He lay back and looked up at the ceiling, smiling as he heard the front door closing. He turned and hugged me at the sound of a car starting up and driving off.

`You've done this before!' I whispered.

`Not often.'

I leaned forwards and kissed him and put my arms round him, but he pushed them back.

`Breakfast,' he said and jumped out of bed, leaving me somewhat bemused as he pulled on a dressing-gown and raced downstairs. I got up, washed, dressed and followed him.

I learned several things about him, over coffee and toast. The most important thing, perhaps, was non-verbal. He looked at me and he smiled and chatted, but he sat at the other side of the table from me; he didn't touch or kiss me or give me knowing looks. I might have been a mere acquaintance rather that someone he'd had sex with and slept with the previous night. He didn't seem embarrassed, or to regret what we'd done, it was more that he appeared to have forgotten it, or to see it as irrelevant. He poured me coffee and told me about himself.

He was unemployed, just eighteen, not enjoying living at home but unable, at present, to decide what to do with himself.

114

`My parents leave me alone,' he said. `I can do what I like, get in as late as I like. They've learned to leave me alone. I have a terrible temper you see, or used to have. They gave up trying to tell me what to do, one day, just like that, after I'd shouted the house down.'

I wanted to jump into bed with him again, but we ended up going out for a walk. We went to the park and wandered down past the benches that were dedicated to this person and that. Ian was curiously unphysical, but this was intriguing in a way, and I was determined not to ruin everything by pushing things too fast.

`I loved that,' he whispered to me at one point, `I loved sleeping with you but not having to have sex with you. That's the best thing, lying close to someone, isn't it?'

I looked at him, at his open face, and wanted to drag him back to bed, right then, and make love to him.

`It's nice,' I muttered, `but it isn't everything.'

There was a café in the park, by the river, where we had lunch looking out over the water, at the birds and the weeping willows. After that we sauntered back to Ian's place via Pug's, where I stopped off to explain – to lie – about where I'd ended up after the party. Once back at Ian's place, he said, `Let's go to bed.'

I agreed enthusiastically and we went upstairs.

`Please,' he said as we went into his room, `let's not have sex. Let's lie side by side. Let's take our clothes off and lie side by side and not do anything except be close.'

It was an odd request, but I went along with it. I lay there, beside him in bed, and he held my hand and I thought: *okay, I can cope with this. I can do this sometimes, so long as I can make love sometimes, too.*

And that was my first twenty-four hours with Ian – a meeting that already had the future wound up within it. And I saw great possibilities ahead. It didn't occur to me, then, though the signals were pretty obvious, that he would try to keep me at arms length, or that he would regularly – habitually – stand me up when we'd arranged to meet.

TWO

The cab arrived late. Addy was already flustered by the time it came, and became even more agitated as it crawled along the busy Saturday afternoon streets. Watching the shoppers cramming the pavements, I felt that the windows through which I was observing them were slides from a microscope – these anonymous bodies were some kind of vibrant impersonal bacteria. Addy, sitting beside me, was still sniffing, but she had stopped crying. She had to reapply the make up round her eyes.

`If you loved Old Jack Butler,' I asked, `why haven't you ever told me about him? You said you'd always tell me everything.'

`I lied. I tell you almost everything. I've told you everything but this.'

`Tell me now.'

She sighed and looked at me for a long time.

`Jack Butler is the only person I've ever loved enough to want to live with. In fact, I did live with him for a time, and it was wonderful.'

`So what happened?'

`Things happened. Your mum made life difficult.'

`My mum!'

`Yes, well, we were closer in those days.'

Adeline looked even more tragic at this, as she thought her way back into her story. I loved the sighing look that shrouded her beautiful face whenever she dipped into the past.

`Jack was ten years older than me,' she said. `Not that it matters, but that's why I called him Old Jack. He was so handsome, and that was only part of it. I loved him absolutely, I was stuck right in the middle of love. I was scuppered by it; undone. I was helplessly crushed by it.'

She cupped my chin with her hand.

`But you'll be okay. At least you know what you want.'

I could see by her face that she had said everything she was going to say on the subject of Old Jack – for the time being at least. I settled back and tried to imagine Addy in love. It was a strange thought, but fitting. I'd never wondered about her lovers – though I'd assumed she'd had them. We never talked about *them. We talked about mine, though. I'd told her of my first kiss with Marc; my first date with Lenny. I didn't tell her the first time I did IT – but she guessed anyway.*

Now, whilst Addy was being so open with me, I decided to ask a question that had hung between us for years.

'Addy, why does mum hate you?'

'Don't be stupid,' she replied. 'Laura doesn't hate me.'

'Yes she does. She always leaves the house before you come to get me. Why is that? She's the last person to miss out on a chat and a gossip with people she knows. But she never talks to you – she never talks about you either, and never asks if I've enjoyed myself with you. Why is that?'

'It's all so complicated. All I can say is that things were different, once, and even when they went sour, she still trusted me to look after you. Remember that. Whatever she may feel now, and for whatever reason, at least she still trusts me.'

Adeline's face fluttered with emotion and, in our wonderful connected way, I realised.

'Mum hates you because of Old Jack Butler!'

'Very clever,' Addy murmured. 'Now be quiet. We're nearly there.'

✳ ✳ ✳ ✳ ✳

I got in from school one Friday – a few days after my fracas with Samantha – and Becky was there, sitting drinking coffee and chatting with my mother, who was between jobs once more. Becky looked shy and nervous, her pale eyes alight with conspiracy. If only she hadn't been here, now, then perhaps I might have liked her. Mum said, 'She's staying to dinner, Paul, I've just invited her.'

'Hello Paul,' she said. 'I was passing on my way home from school.'

'I see you've found an extremely long route home, then,' I said. Mum glared at me.

I had arranged to see Ian that evening and Becky's unexpected presence made it difficult for me not to detest her. Ian and I saw each other only once or twice a week as it was, which wasn't nearly enough for me, especially as

117

we most often spent that time being *close* and holding hands and maybe kissing a little, if that. And what made it worse was the fact that he hadn't turned up the previous week. I'd phoned him the following day whilst his parents were out, and he'd sounded earnest and concerned, and he'd apologised, saying, `I'll *definitely* be there on Friday.'

I was beginning to think that if only I could see more of Ian, then perhaps I could thaw him in some way. I knew he wasn't indifferent to me, but I couldn't understand his reluctance about sex. It was a concern that fascinated me, and made me want to see him even more. Becky's presence meant that I'd have to stand him up, which rankled and made me silent, though I was also aware that it would serve him right.

`For God's sake Paul,' mum said, `brighten up will you and scrub these potatoes.'

`How was school?' Becky asked.

`Boring,' I lied, and thought to myself: *I don't want to dislike you, but I don't know if I can help it.*

`Don't ask Paul about school,' mum said. `He won't talk about it. He doesn't with me, anyway. He thinks I won't know what he's talking about.'

`Mum . . .'

`I would never have been able to get A levels,' she went on, `even if I'd wanted to, which luckily I didn't.'

`Don't say that, mum.'

Becky sat there and looked at me, smiling smugly, and jumped slightly when Duncan crashed through the door looking darkly angry. He stopped short when he saw Becky and looked round at mum. Whatever dynamic of anger had been whirling inside him seemed to click into neutral gear, so that although the anger didn't stop or go away, it ceased to show on the surface.

`Hello Becky,' he said.

`She's come round for dinner,' mum told him.

`Good.' He looked at me as if waiting for confirmation.

`I didn't ask her,' I said.

`Becky, love,' mum said, `could you take these through and lay the table next door.'

118

Becky took the cutlery and left the room. Mum came over to me and smacked me across the top of the head.

`You!' she hissed. `It never hurt anyone to be polite.'

`But I *didn't* ask her.'

`Mind,' said Duncan, as though with that one word he was both warning me and explaining to me what he might do if I didn't conform to his concept of good behaviour.

`Just because you're bright doesn't mean you're better,' mum said. `It doesn't mean you can be rude.'

`It doesn't mean you have to be stuck-up,' Duncan said. `You're not so brilliant, my boy. Not by a long chalk.'

`I am *not* your boy,' I said quietly.

I could see by Duncan's strained jaw that he was only refraining from hitting me because Becky was next door – which was, of course, why I'd felt able to say it.

Dinner was another one of our tawdry affairs. We sat at the table, which was usually left unused at meal times – we almost always ate whilst watching television, neatly getting round the problem of finding conversation, which was nigh impossible, usually. Becky, it turned out, was at the same school that my mother had gone to, and a number of the staff were still there from her time. They talked about that for a while, but it soon petered out.

Eventually even Becky became diffident in the face of silence. She sat there whilst Duncan gathered up the dishes, and when he left the room, mum leant forward and thrust two £5 notes into my hand.

`Go out for a drink or something, you two,' she said. `Go on, I can afford it. We'll stop in and watch television.'

Becky looked questioningly at me. I shrugged slightly.

`Okay,' I said, and stood slowly as though my knees had become calcified from boredom. I went through and got our coats, and then we left.

`Are all your dinners as bad as that?' she asked.

`Yes,' I told her, `or worse.'

`Poor you.'

She took my hand in hers, but I let it drop.

`Where shall we go?' she asked.

`I'm meeting a friend at the Black Horse in twenty

minutes.'

Her face was inscrutable.

`Well,' she said, `I guess that's where we're going, then.'

It was only five minutes walk and when we got there, I paused on the doorstep.

`Look, Becky,' I said, `I have nothing against you, but this is stupid. There's no way that this is going to lead to anything.'

`Why not?'

`Because it just couldn't ever work.'

`Yes it could.'

`Why?'

`Because I love you,' she said, and walked through the door.

I followed her in, sighing at the ceiling, and offered her a drink. I would be polite to her this evening, and then I would make sure she was never invited into our house again. I leaned against the bar and surveyed the customers. There was no sign of Ian, but there were a number of other gay people there (this being the nearest thing to a gay pub in our town, albeit discreet to the point of invisibility).

`Who is your father?' Becky asked as we sat down with our drinks – Molsen for me and Diamond White for her – `do you know him?'

`No,' I said. `Mum was only sixteen when she got pregnant. It wasn't a lasting affair.'

`A year younger than me,' said Becky. `It makes you think.'

`Yes,' I said. `Yes, it does.'

The door of the pub swung open and Ian came in wearing a well cut dark coat with the collar turned up. He crossed over to us and looked questioningly at me.

`Ian, this is Becky; Becky, Ian.'

Becky nodded and said, `I've seen you around. You're the one that Melanie Arnold fancies the pants off.'

`I didn't know you knew Mel,' I said.

`I know her through Samantha.'

`Can I offer you a drink?' Ian asked, looking shuttered, suddenly; remote and offended that I had turned up with

120

someone else.

We both accepted and he went to the bar. I got up and followed him.

`Look,' I said, `I didn't mean to bring Becky, she turned up at my house and mum made me bring her out for a drink.'

Ian looked as though this was a poor excuse.

`You should have got rid of her,' he said.

`It's not that easy.'

`Oh, isn't it?'

We carried the drinks over to the table, and as we sat down, Ian took me in his arms and kissed me on the lips. He lingered far longer than he would have if we'd been on our own, and he continued to lean against me once he'd disengaged from our embrace, drawing some approving looks from other people in the bar.

`We're together,' he said to Becky. `Didn't Paul tell you that he had a boyfriend?'

`No,' said Becky. `No, as a matter of fact, he didn't.'

`That wasn't very fair of him.'

`No, it wasn't,' she said, `though perhaps I should have guessed.'

We sat in silence as we sipped our drinks. Ian smiled at me and patted Becky's hand. She looked down at his extended fingers and then stood up abruptly.

`Um,' she said, `I've got an awful lot of homework to do. I'd better get off.'

Ian said some idle pleasantry as she departed and then beamed at me.

`Easy,' he said.

`But is it true?'

`What?'

`That I'm your boyfriend.'

`Yes, of course. Why? Don't you want to be?'

`Yes, but I thought that being a boyfriend meant more than going out for drinks a couple of times a week. Meant more than sitting around saying how much we like each other.'

Ian swiftly put his fingers to my lips.

121

`Shh,' he said. `Don't take things too fast. Give me time. I can't give you what you want all at once – it's not the way I am. I can only do these things in my own time.'

`When can we make love again?' I asked quietly.

`When do you want to make love?'

`Whenever I see you.'

`You see how much pressure you put me under? How should I respond to that?'

`I don't know.'

`As a matter of fact,' he said, `my mum and dad are out this evening, until midnight at least. Why don't we go back to my place and jump into bed?'

`Okay.'

He smiled his great hectoring grin and said, `Then let's go!'

`By the way,' he added as we walked. `You can't phone me at home during the daytime anymore. Our last bill was *huge* because I've been phoning these 0898 numbers and chatlines. Dad's got himself an answerphone and he locks the phone away during the day.'

We went back to Ian's place, and we got into his bed and we made love and I held his fragrant body in my arms and he was lively and laughing and serious, and I thought how beautiful he was and how wonderful it would be when we could be like this all the time.

✳ ✳ ✳ ✳ ✳

News travels so fast it makes you dizzy. By break time the following day, everyone at school knew about me and Ian – I mean *everyone*. Pug looked dismissively at me, as though I'd betrayed his heterosexual trust or something, and Mel – Mel could hardly bring herself to sneer, she was that close to tears. It wouldn't have been tactful to say to her, `It isn't my fault, Mel, that he loves me and not you.' In her book, I was the culprit, I was the villain who had dragged Ian, kicking and screaming, from the heavenly prospect of her arms.

Curiously, I felt privileged to be the object of smutty

122

innuendo and lame jokes. It was the result of envy, I knew, rather than sincere disapproval. I was doing something out of the ordinary, and whatever anyone may or may not have felt about my sexual inclinations, there was a pleasing irony in the fact that the girls had wondered volubly which one of them was most likely to seduce Ian. It had never occurred to them that a seduction had already been achieved, that I was the one seduced, and that I had been in their midst even as they schemed.

After school I went home feeling somehow *enhanced* by the gossip of others. I was unprepared to find Becky there again, sitting with mum and Duncan in the front room.

`I just came round,' she said, `to thank your mum for giving you the money to take me out last night. We had a great time, didn't we?'

I looked carefully at her expression, trying to divine exactly why she was here, why she was talking to mum and Duncan, and why she was trying to get me to corroborate a lie.

`Yes,' I said slowly, `the evening turned out a lot better than I'd expected.'

`Perhaps this will help to stop all these rumours,' she said with an extremely nasty smile.

`What rumours?' Duncan wanted to know.

`Oh, you know, *rumours*,' she told him, and looked up at me. I could see in her eyes that she was waiting to see what bargain I might strike to stop her from telling them about Ian.

`What rumours are these, Paul?' mum asked. `I can't imagine there being any rumours about you – you never *do* anything.'

`Absolutely,' I said. `Rumours are fickle things. They don't respect the truth and they don't respect integrity. In fact, all they do is demean those who believe them.'

`Unless they happen to be true,' Becky said.

`I don't like secrets,' Duncan muttered. `What is this, Paul?'

`Nothing,' I told him.

`Nothing?'

`Yes, Duncan. Nothing.'

`Watch it,' he warned.

`Don't use that tone with Duncan,' mum told me.

`Or I'll give you a hiding,' Duncan added. `Rumours or no rumours.'

`Look,' said mum, `I don't know what this is all about, but I've got to make a start on the tea. Do you want to stay, Becky?'

`No, thanks Mrs Sandford, I have to go.'

She got up and made a fuss of putting on her coat. I showed her to the door.

`So?' she asked as I let her out. `Are we going to go for a drink together soon?'

`What if I say no?'

`What if I tell your mum and Duncan about you and Ian? Duncan isn't the sort of man I'd like to see angry, especially if I was the one he was angry with.'

`What if I told you that you were a self-righteous, self-serving, power-hungry bitch?'

`You'd be right,' she smiled. `How about Friday?'

*****

I remember the time I told Addy that I was gay. I was sixteen and had recently met this guy called Marc, at a party – another of Mel's do's actually – who had dragged me off for a snog beside the hydrangeas. I'd been pleased, flattered and keen to go all the way. It turned out that he'd expected me to rebuff him, and my ardour unmanned him completely. However, curiosity sparked by this incident, I soon found myself noticing when boys looked at me in a certain way. One such person was Lenny, a friend of Pug's, who was into tennis and swimming – two sports I have never had any interest in, but which I suddenly took up with enthusiasm. I was hopeless at tennis, which meant that Lenny had the chance to do some coaching. It wasn't long before we went for a drink and drifted into having sex.

What made it something of an anticlimax for me was the fact that I quite disliked Lenny by the time we ended up in bed. He was physically arrogant as well as beautiful, and was absolutely certain that he wasn't gay. He was just experimenting. I thought his delusion pathetic and told him so, which led to acrimony and my sudden disinterest in both of his chosen sports. Lenny refused to talk to me again, and that was that. Pug never found out, and a year later, aged eighteen, Lenny got engaged to a waitress call Ellen.

These sexual fumblings, whilst they confirmed my inclinations, also confused me. I thought that sex was going to be wonderful and was angry to discover that this wasn't necessarily the case. So, I went to see Addy.

I'd realised early on that Addy was perceptive. She looked at the world in a different way to most people. She valued integrity far higher than conformity and wasn't afraid to say so. I knew that I couldn't confide in any of my school friends (I could easily guess how Pug would react), and I couldn't say anything to mum or Duncan because I'd heard them sneering, in the most unpleasant way, at that sort of thing when it cropped up on tv.

Not only was Addy my confidante, she was also an entity from another world. Not my world of home and homework, and school, and going to the pub on Friday nights; Addy was separate from that. She helped me get a perspective on it all by being outside it. So I went to her and told her that I had slept with Lenny, that I hadn't enjoyed it, but that I knew what I was and what I wanted.

`So why look so miserable?' she'd asked.

`Why shouldn't I look miserable?' I said. `So many people would hate me if I told them this.'

`People hate very easily,' she said. `Take it as a compliment. It means that they are ignorant, that's all, and that you have risen above their ignorance.'

`So what do you think I should do?'

`About what?'

`About wanting to go and have sex with boys.'

`I think you should have sex with boys.'

`As simple as that?'

`Why not?'

`It feels so much more complicated.'

125

`It is and it isn't,' Addy said. `It doesn't matter who you love, so long as you love within your principles. Apart from that, it's nobody's business.'

She gave me a hug to emphasise her point and I felt a lump in my throat.

`I love you, Addy.'

I had expected surprise at least, but she seemed to have known, or to have expected this, and all she did was smile and hug me again and say what a lot of happiness there was for people if only they could learn to love right.

* * * * *

One evening, soon after the news was out and I was getting used to being recognised as the school faggot, I came home and found the place empty. There was a note from mum on the table: STARTED WORK AT THE WORKINGTON ROAD DISCOUNT FOODMART TODAY. BACK AROUND EIGHT. DINNER ON TABLE.

Ian's mum worked at the Discount Foodmart, too – I wondered if mum knew that. Her note was on top of two packets of microwaveable curry. I took one of them and heated it up, ate quickly, and then started on my homework. At seven I went through to watch *Top of the Pops*. As I was sitting there, Duncan came in. I could hear him tearing at the wrapper of his curry and the clunk of the door of the microwave as he put it in. Over the beat of the music, I listened for the pinging of the timer. He bashed around with plates and cutlery. I heard the *pfft* of a beer can being opened, and then, once the timer had announced his meal, he brought it through on a tray.

I've seen him angry before, I mean, *angry*, but tonight it was awesome. He had a glow to his cheeks that seemed to radiate the heat of his fury. He sat down with his food, then picked up the tv control and switched channel to some programme about the migration of birds.

`I was watching that,' I said.

He didn't answer, just thrust a forkful of curry into his mouth.

126

`Go and do your homework,' he said.

I watched as a bayful of huge white birds took to the air.

`I said go and do your homework.'

`It's okay, I'll watch this.'

Duncan raised his hand, but his tray prevented him from hitting me. I knew, however, that on this occasion I should do as he said. I could see the strain behind his eyes.

I went into the kitchen, made myself some coffee, and then got down to work. After ten minutes or so, Duncan came through and put his tray on the draining board. He turned to me and, reaching out one of his long arms, he struck me across the side of my head, so hard that I nearly overbalanced on my chair.

`That,' he said, `is for the shame you've brought on your mother and me.'

`What?'

He punched me hard on the shoulder and I half fell to the ground, my chair skittering across the floor behind me. I grabbed the side of the table to steady myself.

`Do you know what they've been saying at work?' he said, pushing me on the back as I turned to pick up my chair.

`No,' I said, `how could I?'

I straightened up and turned to him. There was something, I think, in the way I looked at him then – so confused and appalled at this violence and its unfathomable motive – that made him lose rational command of his body. I could see his control snapping, saw it in the intense way he clamped his jaw and in which the inner light of his eyes was quite suddenly extinguished. His fist caught me full in the mouth and I staggered back, crashing against the sideboard with a thump.

`You fucking pansy,' he hissed. `You . . . ' But he had no more words in him. He used his fists instead of words, and they were as eloquent as anything I have ever experienced in my life. They spoke his hate and anger as clearly as they spoke of his shame. I raised my hands to my face to protect myself as best I could, and felt blow after blow, on my head and shoulders and arms and chest, and as I slipped to the

127

floor, I felt his boots as he kicked me, and I heard his ragged breaths and his sobbing.

The door opened and mum came rushing in, breathless.

`Duncan!' she screamed, `Duncan!' and she tried to pull him away as I lay in a foetal position on the blood-smeared tiles. She was too light to be able to pull him off me, but her presence was enough. The blows stopped. I lay immobile, whilst Duncan gasped for breath.

`What is going on!' mum shouted. `What is happening in this house? Tell me, for God's sake. Tell me!'

But as I began to uncurl, I saw Duncan shrug at Laura in his heavy, slightly uncoordinated way, and walk from the room, shoulders bowed as though exhausted.

`Paul,' she whispered, kneeling beside me, `Paul, are you alright? What happened? What did you do?'

I pushed her hand away. I realised, perhaps because of the pain, that I was alone. There was no one here who could comfort me.

`I'm okay,' I whispered. `I just need to go to the toilet.'

She helped me upstairs, sagging as I leaned against her, but I wouldn't let her come into the bathroom. She went downstairs, strained, confused. I sat on the edge of the bath and looked at the floor and remembered what Addy had said to me about how much happiness life could hold. I grimaced at my bloody face in the mirror and it seemed that she might have been talking about some kind of fictional tv wonderland instead of real life.

I bathed my face and my ribs, and a nasty scuff on my knee, then dressed carefully and crept down the stairs to collect my coat. I paused by the kitchen door. I could hear Duncan from the front room.

`I had to do it, Laura,' he was saying. `He's got to learn that some things are wrong.'

And then I walked into the dusk.

✳ ✳ ✳ ✳ ✳

I walked to Ian's house, limping slightly. A pain throbbed at my temple and I could feel a cut weeping gently beside my eye. I'd never met Ian's parents – didn't know what they were like. Disapproving, presumably, or else there would have been no need for secrecy.

When I reached the house – a characterless detached Seventies affair – it was preternaturally quiet. I could see the blue flicker of light from the tv reflected against the far wall of their front room, whose curtains had yet to be drawn. I rang the bell and there was a short silence before I heard footsteps in the hall.

I presumed that the woman who opened the door was Ian's mother. She gasped when she saw my battered face and, pausing, looked back over her shoulder as though expecting reinforcements of some kind. She had no doubt who I was, though she was unsure about how to react to my presence on her doorstep.

`Richard,' she called. `Ian.'

Ian appeared first, almost falling over in his hurry to get to the door before his father, who was close behind.

`Paul . . . ' he said in a half-strangled whisper.

But that was all he managed before his father elbowed him out of the way.

`Right,' he said to me, `I'm warning you. Leave my son alone. You're not welcome here. Go upstairs, Ian. Now.'

Ian didn't move.

`I said now!'

Ian looked carefully at me as he turned to obey. His look was obviously meant to convey a specific message, but I couldn't understand what it was.

You have no idea how difficult you've made things for Duncan and me,' he said. `Coombes isn't the most open-minded of places and rumours have a nasty habit of sticking around for a long time. This whole situation might have been easier to deal with if it wasn't for how we found out – everyone at work knows about it, and it didn't take them long to tell us. I know that you're not entirely to blame – it's as much Ian's fault as yours – but as parents we try to set an example. I won't have you seeing him again. Understand?'

`Please, Mr Levenson, can't I just speak to Ian for a minute?'

`No. Now, get off home.'

`Richard,' Ian's mother whispered, `let me just clean him up a bit in the kitchen first.'

`No, Liz. His mother can do that for him.'

Mrs Levenson looked over Mr Levenson's shoulder with an imploring look of apology, but there was nothing she could do, so she shrugged and turned away. Mr Levenson closed the door, leaving me standing there with the frosted double-glazed panel only inches from my face. I turned and sat on the doorstep. What else could I do? I didn't feel able to go home. I sat and watched as the curtains were swiftly drawn in the front room.

The evening was warm, so I continued to sit on the tiled step. In the dark I could see the miniature firs that stood behind the gate posts. They seemed to punctuate the limitations of my world. I was sitting in an unwelcoming space, but Ian was in his room in the house behind me, so this was where I wanted to be. The sitting room curtains twitched a short time later and I saw Mrs Levenson peering out into the darkness. A minute or two later the door opened behind me. I didn't bother to turn.

`Go away,' said Mr Levenson. He didn't sound angry any more, just embarrassed that I was sitting there. `Go away,' he said again. `There's no point you staying here. Ian's not going to come out.' And then he quietly closed the door.

I remained where I was, waiting for some idea about what to do and where to go. But my mind remained blank – and so I sat on.

After a long time, I don't know how long, the door opened again and Mrs Levenson put her hand on my shoulder.

`Come in,' she said. `Let me see to you.'

I stood slowly, painfully – I was already becoming stiff from my beating – and followed her into the kitchen where she sat me at the table and got a basin of hot water and a cloth, and began to clean my face.

`They're not too bad,' she said. `I'll put plasters on the worst cuts. Hold on.'

I kept on expecting Ian to appear in the doorway, but he didn't. I sat still whilst Mrs Levenson attended to me and then I followed her to the door.

`You'd better do as my husband says, and go home,' she said. `You've had enough trouble as it is.'

I nodded dumbly and walked down the path to the road. Once there, I didn't know which way to turn, so I leaned against the gatepost instead. I felt even more injured than I had before, with the stinging of my cuts and the prickly feeling of sticking-plaster against my skin. I became aware of time passing in the same way that a person might watch traffic go by – it was there, I could experience it as a linear phenomenon, but it was external to me.

I was still no nearer making a decision about what to do and where to go, when I felt the first tears on my cheek. I'd had no advance warning that I was about to cry, and even as the tears flowed, I didn't feel any different.

I felt Ian's hand on my shoulder.

`Come on,' he whispered, `let's get out of here.'

I stood and he embraced me.

`Duncan,' he choked. `What has that bastard done to you?'

`I'm okay. It's okay.'

`You're cold. Let's go.'

`Where?'

`Addy's?'

`But she lives miles away. It's the middle of the night. There aren't any buses.'

`I've got a stack of money,' he said. `We can take a taxi. Or we could stay in a hotel.'

`You're sure you've got enough money for a taxi?'

`Of course,' he smiled. `There's a phone box round the corner. We can call for one from there.'

I leaned against him as we walked.

`Fuck them,' he whispered, more to himself than me. `Fuck them all.' And he hugged me close as we walked and it seemed then, for a moment, that the future would be fine if we could just go on like this.

In the taxi he dozed against me whilst the seconds ticked

on to 3.30 a.m. on the clock. The urban landscape outside was eerily familiar to me, but there was something false about the deserted streets, as though this were some dehumanised facsimile of the place where I had lived all my life. I looked carefully at Ian, now, as he sat, looking tired and vulnerable.

`Where were you on Friday?' I asked.

He opened his extraordinary eyes, then, suddenly wide awake.

`Don't be angry,' he said, quickly. `I couldn't make it, that's all.'

`I'm not angry now,' I said. `But I was. What's the point of making arrangements if you don't stick to them?'

`Shh,' he said. `I love you. That's all that matters right now.'

When we got there, the house in which Addy had her flat was dark. I fumbled for some time before I could work out which was her doorbell and we waited for such a long time after I'd rung it that I assumed she was either not in, or frightened to come down.

`Who is it?' she asked, eventually, through the door. When I replied, she rattled with the locks and chains.

`Paul, my God, what are you doing here at this time? And Ian! Come in, come in.'

She ushered us upstairs and sat us in the cool sitting room whilst she filtered some coffee for us, pausing to splash some whisky into it before handing it over.

`Okay,' she said, `I know things are bad. I've worried for a long time that Duncan might do this, but I always felt that I was imagining things – overreacting.'

`They found out about us,' I said.

`Yes,' she said. `But don't talk about it now. You both look shattered. Let me make up a bed for you in here. We can talk about it in the morning.'

I sipped my coffee and leaned against Ian whilst Adeline bustled around us. For the first time that night, I began to feel sleepy – because, for the first time, I felt safe.

When the mattress was positioned, Addy straightened and turned to us.

132

`Okay, boys, you can do the bedding yourselves.'

She left us to it. Together we put the sheets and blankets on, and then I lay down with Ian and he took my face in his hands and kissed my cuts and bruises one by one.

`You've really been through it,' he said.

`Let's make love,' I replied. `I want to.'

`No,' he said. `I can't. Not now, it's not right. Let's cuddle up and go to sleep. It's better that way – to just hold someone you love. It's the only thing that really matters, to *hold* someone.'

*****

When I woke up, I was aware of several things: that I was hurting all over; that I was late for school; that Addy was in the kitchen cooking us all some breakfast, and that Ian was up already – I could hear him splashing in the bathroom. He came through, towelling his hair and smiling radiantly.

`Hi,' he said, and dumped the wet towel on my face, then leapt on to the settee where he reclined like a Fifties matinée idol. I grimaced back at him, incapable under the circumstances of managing a genuine smile. He fell forwards from the sofa onto our mattress and turned to me.

`It's all going to be okay,' he laughed. `Who needs families? We'll get through this and then we can be ourselves; together.'

He kissed me as Addy clattered through with plates of food.

`An old fashioned fry-up,' she said. `Let's eat!'

`Here,' Ian said, standing up and throwing an old dressing-gown of Addy's at me. As I tried to get up, I winced with pain. My ribs felt as though they were on fire. Ian knelt beside me and helped me up. Addy looked at me with a sympathy that was laced with both horror and regret – and guilt, perhaps, though no blame could be attached to her. She moved her chair slightly to make room at the gate-legged table in the window, and poured me a mug of tea.

`I don't suppose there's much point in your going to

school today,' she said. `Though I'm not sure what you should do about going home.'

`It'll be okay,' I said. `At least for a while. Duncan's never been as violent as that before, though he's been close to it. He frightens himself so much when he hits me that he usually goes all quiet and docile for weeks afterwards. I'll go back and be careful, and if I can last until after my exams, then maybe I can find a job and move out. It's only a couple months.'

`If you're sure.'

I nodded over a mouthful of fried bread.

`We'll be careful,' said Ian. `We can meet on neutral ground and then, when Paul's done his exams, we can find a flat somewhere.'

It was the first time he'd mentioned us living together, and he smiled shyly at me as he mentioned it, as though he was making a proposal of marriage or something, and he leaned forwards over the table and put his hand on mine.

`But what about *your* home life?' Addy asked him.

`Oh, me,' he sighed. `I despise my parents, and in their own loving way they despise me. Dad isn't pissed off because he's found out that I'm gay, he's livid because he was made fun of by his colleagues at work. He shows his disapproval alright, but at least he doesn't beat me up.'

He squeezed my hand as he said this, and then kissed my fingers.

`Look,' Addy said to me, `I've got to get off for work. Stay here for as long as you like. Let yourself out with the spare keys – they're by the phone. You can give them back to me tomorrow when I come over to see you; or better still, you can keep them, in case you ever come round when I'm not in. Stay all day if you like,' she said as she shrugged herself into her coat.

I stood and went to her, and hugged her gently.

`I love you, Addy,' I said. `What would we do if we didn't have you to help us out?'

`The feeling,' she said, `is mutual. Now, look, you've smudged my make-up. Never mind, *au revoir*!'

After she'd left, we made more tea and then lay back on

the bed and Ian hugged me. I couldn't hide the fact that I had an erection, but I was careful not to make any kind of advance for fear of another refusal. Ian noticed it and ignored it for a while; then he broke away and leaned down to kiss the tip.

`I'm sorry,' he whispered to it, and stroked it for a moment, and then he stretched alongside me again.

`Why is it?' he said, `that there has to be sex at all? Why can't people just love each other without ever having to involve their bodies?'

I couldn't answer this. I had no wish to separate love and sex and was confused as to why he might want to do so himself. I lay back and looked up at the cracked artex of the ceiling and felt almost incapacitated by my unrequited lust.

✳ ✳ ✳ ✳ ✳

I got home in the early afternoon. The house was empty, but even so, for some reason, I crept upstairs. I ran a bath and lay in it for ninety minutes or so, topping it up every now and then with more hot water. It was mesmeric to lie there, and curiously comforting.

When I eventually got out, it wasn't because I wanted to, but because I recognised that it would be disempowering to be still bathing when Duncan came home. I needed to be dressed, at least, and preferably working hard at my studies. I dried carefully, took my plasters off, and washed my face meticulously. Already some of the swelling had gone down and my face looked less ravaged, less tormented.

I set out my books and files, but that was only for show. I sat at the table and read *Macbeth*.

Duncan was the first to come home. He opened the door quietly, almost timidly, and, after removing his jacket, went through to watch the news on tv without even a glance at me. Laura came home about half-an-hour later. She looked shyly at me as she cleared a space for her bag of groceries.

`Hello, love,' she said. `Alright?'

`Yes mum.'

135

`Hard at work? Good.'

She put the kettle on and called through to ask Duncan if he wanted some tea. I felt as if I was on stage. I was a character in a badly written play. I was false, fictional – choked with things that I ought to be saying, but instead all that came out of my mouth were banalities.

I asked mum how it was, working at the Foodmart.

`Oh,' she said, `you know. Filling shelves is tough. But I can manage. At least I can get discounts, and some of the damaged stock is free.'

`Have you met Ian's mum. She works there too.'

`Shh,' said mum. `Don't mention Ian in this house, especially not when Duncan's home.' She paused for a moment. `Yes, I did know she works there. She's the check-out manageress. Snobby cow, won't even talk to the likes of me.'

She said this quietly, as though acknowledging that she should be talking about my battered face; about where I had been the previous night. But we talked instead about what we were about to eat (chicken in cook-in chasseur sauce followed by past-the-sell-by-date baked cheesecake from the delicatessen section).

After I'd cleared the table and mum had served the meal, Duncan came through. We sat in silence whilst we ate and it felt as if *I* was the one who'd committed a crime. It was as if I was out on probation, and mum and Duncan were treating me with special care in case I should go berserk again. They kept on glancing at each other as though they were the ones who had done nothing wrong.

I ate my cheesecake, which was delicious, and then I stood up.

`I'm going out,' I said.

I looked from mum to Duncan to see what reaction they would give. Duncan just stared down at his plate.

`Where?' mum asked.

`Just out.'

`With your friends from school?' She looked at me, pleading with her eyes for me to say yes, for me to lie and say yes.

136

`No,' I said, `I'm going to see Ian.'

I saw Duncan's hands tighten where he was holding on to the edge of the table. They were so strained that there was a pale dot on each of his knuckles. Mum looked at me with such hatred, then, that it made me wince inside.

`Well,' she said, trying to sound casual but actually rasping the words in a grotesque whisper, `don't be too late, will you?'

I nodded and went through to the hall to get my jacket.

I had arranged to meet Ian on the corner of Larkshill playground, by the phone box. We'd decided to rendezvous there and, if necessary, wait for up to an hour. If either of us couldn't make it, then we'd phone the call box – whose number Ian had noted – to explain.

I waited for well over an hour before I acknowledged that he would neither show up nor phone. I think I was too numb inside to even really mind that he'd stood me up again. I kept thinking of that morning and how he'd said to Addy that he wanted us to live together, and how he'd whispered, `Fuck them all,' with such sincerity on the way to the taxi the previous night. I stood there and, feeling anaesthetised, turned away and began to walk home. It was still early, but I couldn't bring myself to drop in on people like Mel, or Pug, and so I walked on.

As I walked, I realised I was close to where Becky lived. Perhaps it was something perverse in me, but I couldn't help it. I walked to her house and without thought, without hesitation, I rang her bell.

It took a while before she opened the door, and when she did, she gasped at my bruised face. She stood there and her usual assurance dissolved – her body, so convincingly upright, seemed to sag slightly against the lintel. Her expressive lips puckered as she looked questioningly at me.

`You said "How about Friday",' I told her. `Well here I am.'

`What happened to your face?'

`Duncan had a go at me – about Ian.'

`God,' she said. `I don't know how your mother puts up with that guy.'

137

'Well,' I said, 'are you coming out?'

She thought for a moment.

'Okay. Stay there. I'll get my bomber.'

I waited and was surprised when Becky returned after a moment, without her jacket.

'Look,' she sighed, 'I won't come out, if you don't mind. I don't think you'd be keen to spend time with me if you knew what I've done.'

'Why, what have you done?'

'I told them, Paul. I mean, I told Gerry Deering – he works down at Coombes. He must have told Duncan.'

'Gerry Deering!' I groaned. 'I remember him. He was at my school. If you told him, then *everyone* will know.'

'I know,' she said. 'That's the terrible thing. I knew that even as I told him. That's *why* I told him. It sounds terrible now, but I wanted to hurt you.'

She leaned against the doorframe, unsure what to say next. She was obviously confused and upset by the deceitfulness of her actions, and it occurred to me, then, that if we had met under different circumstances, we would be friends.

'And now you are hurt,' she said, 'I didn't think it would turn out to be so physical.'

'Anyway,' I said, 'I don't care who knows, now. All I wanted was to keep it quiet from mum and Duncan, because I knew that Duncan would fly off the handle. Now that he knows, what difference can it make that everyone else knows too?'

'I suppose you must really hate me.'

'I don't hate you,' I said. 'I don't think I even hate Duncan any more. Isn't that weird? I thought I'd hate him forever, but it hurts to hate – I hadn't realised that, but it does. It's so much easier to be numb inside.'

138

THREE

The last mourners were going into the church when our taxi pulled up. Addy looked across at me as though she was about to tell me something significant. But the moment passed and she picked up her black lace gloves instead.

`Come on,' she said, `let's go. We can sit at the back.'

She paid the driver and then got out, slowly and gracefully. Only the usher was left outside the church and it seemed that Addy was putting on a show just for him. She took my hand and we walked up the short slope together and I thought: SHE LOVED THIS MAN WHO IS DEAD. SHE LOVED JACK BUTLER, AND SHE NEVER TOLD ME.

She looked so beautiful as she walked beside me, her head high, a string of pearls at her throat.

`Hello Adeline,' said the usher. `I was wondering if you would turn up.'

We went into the church, into the echoing space filled with people.

`Who was that man on the door?' I asked as she pulled me down onto one of the pews.

`Just a friend of Jack's,' she said. `Now, shh.'

`I wish you'd told me more about Jack,' I whispered. `I'd like to know.'

`I'll tell you,' she said. `I'll tell you everything, later.'

And as I sat, I noticed that people were turning round to look at Addy. They were turning round, especially the women – who made up about a third of the congregation. They were glancing their curious glances, and nodding and turning back to nudge their neighbours.

The church was full, but the funeral was boring. I'd been to my grandfather's funeral the previous September, so this was nothing new. Death seems so crazy and alien to me. Everyone was crying, so I knew Old Jack must have been a popular guy. Someone in the pew in front of me said how terrible it was that he should have died so young.

✳✳✳✳✳

139

On Saturday – the day after Addy had given me the keys to her flat – she turned up at mid-day as usual. She seemed subdued and shifty, as though mum or Duncan might be lying in wait for her. She took her usual envelope from her bag and put it on the kitchen table.

`What is that?' I asked her. `Why do you always leave a letter for mum?'

`I always have,' she said. `Perhaps it's pointless, but I got into the habit of it and now I can't bring myself to stop. I just give her my bit of news, for what it's worth. She might not be interested – in fact I'm sure she isn't – but she's never actually asked me to stop. It's just another of my many little foibles.'

She put her hand to my cheek.

`You're looking better,' she said. `How's it been with Duncan?'

`I was right,' I said. `He's on his best behaviour. I'm safe. For a while.'

`I don't like you being here.'

`It's not for much longer, Addy. I'll be okay.'

`But will you?' she asked, concerned.

`Of course. Now, come with me. We're meeting Ian in Stewards at one. He wants to see you again, and so I've decided to give you the honour of buying us lunch.'

Addy laughed.

`My pleasure,' she said, `though I worry that you're developing such expensive tastes.'

Stewards was another of Addy's out-of-the-way venues. It was a busy restaurant and so I had thought to book a table. Ian was already waiting outside when we got there, and he took me in his arms and kissed me out there in the car park. Addy beamed her approval.

`How *are* you?' Ian asked. `Your face looks as if it's recovering. Actually, it's quite sexy.'

`In we go,' said Addy.

We were given a table at the window. Our waiter was gay and did not try to hide his pleasure when Ian smiled at me, or held my hand surreptitiously beneath the table. I couldn't resist his quizzical smile, and the touch of his

140

fingers on my thigh.

`I feel so clandestine,' I said, `which makes this all seem much more poignant, somehow.'

`It's so unfair,' Addy murmured, `when people refuse to recognise love in others, just because it's different to how they've experienced it for themselves.'

`But you recognise it,' said Ian. `And that makes a big difference.'

`Does it?' she smiled. `I'm so pleased.'

`How come you're different?' I asked. `How come you never disapproved?'

`You'll find, as soon as you move away from this town, that some places are so different you'll hardly be able to believe it. Your mum and Duncan belong to a dying breed – you'll see. And as for me, well, I've found that love is rarer than you could possibly imagine. The only real crime in this life is to deny love, whatever form it takes.'

✳ ✳ ✳ ✳ ✳

The following Friday, I was at home. I hadn't seen Ian since my meal at Stewards. Usually we arranged our next meeting before we parted, but this time we hadn't and I had been in a strange limbo of expectancy. It had become an unspoken arrangement that we would both be down at The Black Horse on Friday evenings, so I knew I would be seeing him later anyway – but I felt adrift when I was apart from him, which was both pleasant and unpleasant at the same time. I hadn't mentioned Ian to mum or Duncan since the previous Thursday, and Duncan had slipped into a sullen silence with me. He was drinking more than ever these days and his palpable unhappiness actually began to make me feel sorry for him.

The last person I expected to see was Becky, and when she called, I wondered at her motives. Mum was thrilled and darted out into the hall when she saw her coming through the gate.

`Becky! Come in.'

`Hello, Mrs Sandford. I was wondering if I could have a

word with Paul?'

`Of course, please. Would you like a beer?'

`Thanks.'

`Paul!' mum called, though she knew quite well that I could hear her conversation from where I was sitting watching tv. `Becky's here. Duncan, get her a glass of beer.'

I came out into the hall as Duncan went off to the kitchen.

`Come up to my bedroom,' I said, `we can talk there.'

It was interesting to note that, two months before, if I had invited a girl up to my bedroom, mum and Duncan wouldn't have allowed it. Now, however, they were bordering on the triumphant.

`You're honoured by the way,' I whispered, after Duncan had handed her a glass of lager, `he never gives me any of his beer.'

Becky followed me into my room. I reclined on the bed. She sat on the radiator.

`It's tiny in here,' she said. `You must hate it.'

I shrugged.

`Of course,' she said, `you must be wondering why I came.'

`It had crossed my mind.'

She rummaged in her shoulder bag and took out a large envelope.

`I've been wondering whether I should show you these.'

`But now you've decided that you will.'

She handed me the envelope. I opened it and pulled out the contents. There was a bundle of pages that had been cut from magazines, perhaps four or five sheaves, all with three or four pages stapled together. Each sheaf was a different porno photo session, and in each one the model was Ian.

I've seen a few porno mags, and these pictures were standard stuff, starting fully clothed and then graduating through various states of undress to full nudity. In one he was a repairman; in another a window cleaner; in another a milkman. In the magazines he was called John, Rod, Lance . . . At the end of the pages there was a number of cards for newsagents windows, or phone boxes. *Luke, 18, young masseur, gives full body service in private flat*; and a cut-out

142

from a gay listing section – *Christopher, 18, dark hair, blue eyes. Intelligent, sensual, athletic and horny. Complete service in private flat. Mobile: 0860 691 ___.*

`He does it for money,' Becky said. `He's a prostitute.'

Why wasn't it a shock? I'm not sure. Of course, it explained why he had stood me up so many times. I thought, too, of how he regarded sex and nudity as a chore. He had always preferred to hug me rather than make love to me. Was it because he'd made sex so impersonal that it no longer had anything to do with love?

`How do you know he's a prostitute?' I asked. `This isn't his phone number.'

`Don't be naive, Paul.'

`Where did you get these from, anyway?' I asked.

`That doesn't matter,' she said. `I just thought you ought to know, that's all.'

`Okay, so now I know. Great.'

`Look,' she said, `I'm doing this for you as well, you know. You ought to know what you're involved with.'

`Thanks a lot. It's good to know you're so altruistic.'

`Yes, well . . . ' she paused for a moment before looking across at me. `You're right to be angry and sarcastic. I'm sorry.'

`I wonder if his parents know?' I thought aloud, `I wonder why he's still living at home?'

`His parents,' she said, `won't see anything, because they know that if they look too hard they'll see too much. Isn't that the way with so many parents? Isn't that the way with your mum and Duncan? Samantha's known you were gay for years. She only set me up with you as a nasty prank.'

`Samantha's always been good at nasty pranks. She gets it from Aunt Christine.'

`Only this prank turns out not to have been funny at all. Not even for Samantha. It's ruined our friendship.'

`You're better off without her as a friend,' I said. `I should know.'

`It's laughable,' she said. `I've dreamed, from the first time I met you, of being asked up into your bedroom. And now I'm here.'

143

`Funny, huh?'

`Ha sodding ha.'

She pulled her hair behind her ear and looked down at the carpet, then up at me. She smiled tentatively, and I couldn't help smiling back.

*****

I remember talking to Addy the previous year, shortly after losing my virginity to Lenny.

`Whoever it is that you love,' she'd said, `the first thing you have to be sure of is that it is love. That's the hardest thing – to differentiate between love and infatuation. Then, if it is love, you have to lose yourself completely. That's the second hardest thing – or first equal more likely. You have to go with your heart, because if you don't, your head will ruin everything.'

I lay back on my bed after Becky had gone and tried to decide whether I loved Ian, and if so, what his secret life meant to me. Becky had left the buff envelope on my windowsill and I reached for it. I would be seeing Ian later that evening and I wondered how I was going to feel.

The photos of Ian were poorly shot and did him little justice. They made him into just another anonymous *lad*. I couldn't work out at first what it was that was missing from the pictures, but then I realised that it was the specific aura that he created with his movements and expressions. There was no sign of his intense physical grace or his ability to convey so much with a mere glance. His celebrated eyes lacked their usual lustre, and the absence of contrast in the photos flattened his contours. I looked at them and thought: *I am looking at a complete stranger*.

I remembered him telling me that he had a stack of money the night we took a taxi to Addy's place. I hadn't even thought to question why he had it, or where it had come from. It had never occurred to me to question Ian about anything. It was enough that he seemed to love and need me.

But knowing these new things about him changed the way I saw him. I couldn't define how this change affected me, or how it was going to manifest itself. All I was aware of was that I looked at these photographs and they told me that Ian was not who I thought he was. So what did that make him? I had no idea.

In the end, I took a couple of pound coins and went downstairs.

'Where are you off to?' mum said as I picked up my jacket.

'I'm off for a drink with Mel and Becky,' I told her, getting it right this time. Duncan didn't say anything.

I went to the phone box a couple of blocks away and called the mobile number. The phone rang for a long time before anyone answered. When it did, the voice at the other end was abrupt.

'Yup?'

'Hi,' I said, 'can I speak to Christopher please?'

'Oh,' the voice softened. 'He's not here right now. What did you want him for?'

'I wanted to meet up with him for . . . for a massage.'

'I see. Have you been to see Christopher before?'

'No. I saw his advert in the paper. Um, how much is it?'

'A massage? It's forty pounds, basic. Extras start at ten pounds on top of that.'

'Extras?'

'There's no need to be nervous,' he told me. 'Customers are often nervous, but we're very friendly so there's no need to worry. Now, extras. You can negotiate at the time if you like, but Christopher doesn't do anything heavy, okay?'

'Okay. A massage will be fine.'

'Your name?'

'Andrew Newell.'

'A first name is all we need, Andrew. When do you want to see Chris?'

'Tonight.'

'That won't be possible, I'm afraid. How about tomorrow evening?'

'Fine, great.'

145

'Seven-thirty?'

'Okay.'

'How old are you, Andrew?' he asked.

'Twenty-six,' I replied.

'I thought you sounded young.'

'What's the address?'

'How are you going to pay?'

'Cash,' I said.

The address was in an upmarket part of town, two or three miles away. I thanked the man and hung up. There was something completely unreal about what was happening. I could hardly believe that it could be true – that Ian was doing this.

I went to the Black Horse at the relevant time and Ian was not there. I bought a drink and for the first time I wondered *why* he wasn't there. Was he at that moment 'relieving' someone of their tension by giving them a massage with extras? Did I disapprove of it as a concept, or just the idea of my boyfriend doing it without telling me? *Boyfriend* suddenly seemed an entirely inappropriate label to apply to him.

When Ian did arrive, forty minutes late, he sensed my unhappiness immediately and bought us both a pint before coming to sit down.

'Hi,' he said. 'Sorry I'm late. Don't worry, though, it's not going to be like this for much longer. Once you've done your exams, things'll change.'

'I've never asked you why you're still living at home,' I said.

'For as long as I don't have a job,' he said, 'there isn't much alternative. Of course, I'm not really looking for a job, either. But I will once you're free and we can get far, far away from this town.'

'But you're so well dressed,' I said. 'You always have money.'

'Mum and dad don't charge me rent,' he said, 'you know that. Dad also gives me pocket money – *guilt* money I call it.'

'But he works at Coombes. He can't be earning all that much.'

`He earns a lot more than Duncan,' Ian said, `and mum's got a good job. Anyway, what is this, an inquisition?'

`No. I just wondered.'

`Look Paul, just work hard, get good grades, and then we can fuck off to a place worth living in. Edinburgh, maybe, or Manchester, or we could go off into the middle of nowhere and laze about in a derelict cottage in the hills for a year. Why not? We can do anything we want, once we've got away from home.'

`We could go and live in Glasgow,' I said. `My *single* Uncle Mark lives there. I haven't seen him for years. We could go and stay with him, maybe, and try to find out exactly why he's single. Maybe he isn't single. Maybe he has a lover and he just hasn't told mum or Aunt Christine.'

`Yes,' said Ian, smiling his broad emphatic smile. `Let's go up there sometime and find out.'

`Look,' I said, `why don't we drink up and then go over to Addy's this evening? She's not going to be there so we could have the place to ourselves.'

`No,' said Ian. `Not this evening. I'm tired, and it's a long way. Let's stay here and get pissed. Okay?'

`I don't want to get pissed,' I said. `I want to go to bed with you.'

`There'll plenty of time for that,' he said. `Later.'

* * * * *

The next day Addy came to pick me up. This time she took a larger envelope than usual out of her bag and put it on the table. She ignored my questioning glance and ushered me out of the house.

`How is Ian?' she asked.

`Fine,' I said, wondering briefly if I should tell her what I knew about him. But Addy was so idealistic, I didn't want to spoil her image of him. Besides, I was still trying to work out what my instinctive feelings were – she had always told me to go with my instincts – and it would only muddle me to try and put something into words that was so confusing as a feeling.

We had a somewhat subdued day and Addy tried to wheedle out of me what the matter was, but I kept quiet; telling her only that I had to go somewhere, and borrowing the money for the bus fare.

I was home by six. Mum and Duncan were still not back, so I ate some tomato sauce on toast and left them a brief note before going off to get my bus, which was late as usual, and which dropped me off a good walk from where I had to go. I enjoy walking, and it was warm, so I didn't mind. I got to the place just before seven. It was in a large Victorian house with a Seventies crazy paving parking space and peeling ornamented gables. I went off and wandered around the streets for half-an-hour, wondering – worrying almost – why I didn't feel nervous.

When I went back to the house, I still felt calm. I reached out to press the intercom buzzer for flat five, but my finger stopped a centimetre or so from the button. I stood and looked at my finger, poised there by the buzzer, and wondered what the ultimate outcome would be from pressing it . . . *And what*, I thought, *if it isn't Ian?*

Then I pressed it.

`Hello,' a voice came almost immediately. I recognised it straight away.

`Hi,' I said into the microphone, `it's Andrew. Andrew Newell.'

`Okay, come up. Second floor.'

The door clicked open. I walked in and started up the stairs. It was only then that I realised I hadn't thought of what I was going to say. There was no obvious conversation starter for meeting your lover in the capacity of being a sex client.

The second floor landing had only one door – a heavy, dark-stained wooden door with a hefty lock. As I came to the top of the stairs, someone opened it. And there he was. There we were – standing face to face on the worn carpet of a provincial house – staring at each other. He was wearing jeans and a crisp white T-shirt and looked younger, I thought, without any of his expensive clothes.

In spite of a certain feeling of desperation and rising

148

misery, I managed a slim smile.

`Hello, Christopher.'

`Paul,' Ian whispered, `what are you doing here?'

`I phoned up and booked an appointment.'

`Shit,' he said, and his face crumpled, quite suddenly, into that of a frightened child when it has been caught doing something wrong.

`Are you going to invite me in?' I asked. `Or shall we talk here. Maybe we could go for a walk?'

`You can't come in,' he whispered. `Eddy's inside. My . . . manager.'

`Come for a walk. Or we can go to Addy's, if you like. It's not far from here.'

`Go away, Paul,' he pleaded. `Please.'

`Ian,' I said, `tell me what's happening. What is all this? Why are you doing this?'

`I'll meet you later,' he said. `How about ten-thirty at the Black Horse?'

`No,' I said. `No. Tell me now. This is crazy, Ian. Why didn't you say something to me about it?'

`Oh, yeah, what was I going to say? And anyway, I'm only doing this for a while. When we leave town I'll stop doing this for good.'

`Come with me,' I said. `I've booked you for an hour.'

`*Half* an hour,' Ian said. `That's all you get for forty quid.

`Okay,' I said, `I'll still pay for it.'

`With what?'

`Chris?' came a voice from inside the flat. Ian looked around and fumbled in his pocket, pulled a roll of notes from his pocket and peeled off forty pounds.

`Here,' he whispered, urgently. I took the money, bemused. The man, Eddy, appeared in the doorway – casually dressed, large, powerful.

`What's going on?' he asked. `Who is this?'

`I'm Andrew,' I said. `Andrew Newell.'

`I know him,' Ian said. `He wants me to go for a walk.'

`No way, kid,' he said to me.

`It's okay, Eddy,' Ian told him. `He's okay. I don't mind going for a walk. He'll pay.'

`How old are you?' he asked.

`Eighteen.'

`That's not what you said on the phone. So, you want to go for a walk?'

`Yes.'

`It'll still cost you forty quid.'

`Here,' I said, handing him the money.

`Right,' said Eddy, folding the notes and thrusting them into his back pocket. `You're weird, but that's okay if Chris knows you.'

`I'll just get my jacket,' Ian said. `Then we can go. I don't have anything else on for this evening.'

He went back into the flat and Eddy and I stood on the landing. He smirked at me as I tried to look nonchalant.

`You shouldn't be paying for this shit at your age,' he said. `You should be out having fun. With a face like yours you could go places. Especially in a business like this.'

A cool breath of dislike chilled me, and I looked at the floor. Ian came out wearing a black leather biker's jacket that I hadn't seen before and, taking my elbow, he started down the stairs.

`I'll ring you tomorrow,' he called over his shoulder.

When we were out on the pavement Ian turned and started walking up a slow incline towards a small park. He had his hands in his pockets and looked as though he was in a fugue state. After a while I realised that, unless I spoke, the silence wasn't going to be broken. We reached the park and Ian swung the squeaky gate open and held it for me.

`How long,' I asked. `How long have you been doing this?'

Ian shrugged, and scuffed the mossy gravel of the path.

`What do you do with these people?' I asked. `Apart from massage them.'

He looked away from me and glanced up at the sweeping branches of the beech trees that stretched above us.

`How did you get into this whole thing?' I asked. `I've seen the photos too, you know. Becky gave them to me.'

Ian hunched up his shoulders as though he was cold and pushed his hands deeper into the pockets of his jacket.

150

`How did you meet Eddy?' I asked. `Who is he?'

I realised, as I asked these questions, that Ian wasn't going to answer, or at least not right now. But I couldn't stop asking.

`What's it like? Do you enjoy it? How many times a week do you have sex with a customer? How far do you go with them?'

I could see Ian's expression closing off, gradually, with each question I asked. Eventually, I stopped and sat on one of the warped wooden benches. He sat beside me.

`Shit!' I shouted and punched the wood beside me. Ian put a closed fist to his mouth and began to chew gently on his knuckles. I shook my hand in pain.

`Tell me what to do,' I said. `Tell me what to say to you. How should I react to this, Ian? Because I can't stand you just sitting there saying nothing. What are we going to do? Go on like before, being sweet and innocent and holding hands, and hugging and being close and not making love because you're not ready for it? What does that mean, anyway? Is that why you don't want to make love to me, because you've been too busy fucking around with other people for money? Is that it? You just can't get it up because your dick's too worn out from over-use?'

Ian closed his eyes and started breathing rhythmically, carefully.

`Shit, Ian, I can't stand this. I'm going to get up, now, and I'm going to walk away from you and then that's going to be it. I'm going to go home and I'm going to work hard and get good grades and I'm not going to see you again. It's not that I hate what you're doing – I just don't *understand* what you're doing, and what it's got to do with me. You can go back to your fat businessmen, or whoever it is that you prefer having it off with. Sex isn't everything, as you've said, but it *is* a part of loving someone. I just can't wait round for the odd evening when you've got enough sperm left over to make a generous donation to me.'

I stood up and began walking from the park. I walked slowly, waiting for Ian's footsteps behind me, but there was no sound other than the wind in the branches above

151

me and the distant hum of traffic on the dual carriageway. When I got to the rusty gate I even paused, hoping that he was watching me, and turned to glance back at him. But in the deepening dusk I could see him, still sitting on the bench, looking down at his lap.

I walked for about an hour without having any coherent thoughts. It's incredible that time seems to slow down, to stop almost, and then you find that, contrary to your perception, an hour has passed – ninety minutes – when you thought you'd simply been wandering for a few minutes. Without consciously choosing to, I'd been walking towards the impersonal suburb where Addy lived. Who else could I turn to?

It was just after nine-thirty when I got to her flat. I let myself into the main building using the key that she had given me, and I walked slowly up to her door, banging on it to warn her of my presence, rather than using the key.

There was a rustling for some moments, then the door opened and Addy was standing in the doorway wearing a crimson halter-necked dress. Her hair was piled on her head, a ringlet falling down each cheek, and she looked so glamorous that I could do nothing but cry out and fall, sobbing, into her arms.

`Okay,' she said, ruffling my hair and holding me tight. `Let go. Let it all go.' And she stroked my hair, neck, and shoulders, and she murmured to me as I cried. We stood there for a long time before I could gain control of myself. When my shaking had subsided, she took me by the shoulders and drew me into the flat.

`You go and clean up,' she whispered, propelling me into the bathroom. `I'll get you a drink.'

I stood in front of the basin and looked at myself – bloodshot eyes, a strand of snot on my upper lip, a fading bruise above my right eye from Duncan's beating.

What is happening to me? I thought as I ran some hot water on a luxuriant flannel and started to sponge my face.

After I had washed and splashed cold water on my burning cheeks, I took several deep breaths and, feeling peculiarly emotionless, left the bathroom and went into the sitting-room. Ian was sitting in one of the easy chairs by the fireplace. He looked up shyly as I walked in, then stood up slowly. Addy, who was hovering just inside the doorway, left, closing the door gently behind her.

`I knew you'd come here,' he said. `I've been waiting here for nearly an hour.' He crossed the room and put his arms round me and hugged me.

`I didn't do anything with them,' he whispered. `The most I've ever done is toss them off, or sometimes suck them off through a condom. They've never touched me. Looked, yes, but never touched. Eddy's made sure of that. And I don't do it very often – maybe once or twice a week, that's all. I couldn't bring myself to let them touch me,' he added. `Eddy wanted me to, but we eventually came to an agreement, and he's stuck to it. He's not so bad. He's been good to me at least.'

Addy opened the door and came in with three glasses. I broke off from Ian and we both went to sit down. I sat in the armchair on the other side of the fireplace from him.

`Gin,' she said, `with ice and a little lime juice cordial. Here.'

She handed us a glass each and then sat down on the sofa and began to paint her fingernails carmine red.

`There are a lot worse things in this world than selling sex,' Addy told me, as she concentrated. `But this business isn't for the likes of you – either of you. And it could have been either of you, believe me. Don't get me wrong, I'm not defending Ian, because I think he's been deceitful, and I've told him so.'

She looked hard at me.

`People will do all sorts of things to escape a loveless life. You mustn't judge people by what you yourself have or haven't felt compelled to do. Ian loves you, Paul. I can see that even if you can't right now. You've got to let him learn to show it in actions as well as words. And now,' she said, blowing on her nails, `I must be off. How do I look?'

`Stunning,' I said.

`That,' she smiled, `is the right answer.'

She kissed us both carefully, downed her drink, and

picked up her keys.

`There's more gin in the fridge,' she said, and was gone.

I picked up my glass and took a sip. Ian started to flick through Addy's record collection, eventually picking out an old Janis Joplin LP and putting it on the small portable player. I watched as he did so; as he turned to smile when the needle connected with the crackling vinyl groove.

`Neat, huh?' he said, and came over to kiss me.

`I won't ask you to make love to me,' I said. `I couldn't do it myself tonight. I'm too tired to even want to try.'

Ian slumped beside me on the settee and looked at the ceiling, taking two or three breaths before he spoke.

`Do you want to know how I got into it?' he asked.

`I don't know.'

`I'll tell you. Then at least you won't be able to accuse me of keeping secrets.'

I leaned back in my chair and watched him as he talked.

`I've been all over,' he said. `Dad has worked everywhere. Leeds, Manchester, London, Preston, Chester, Barnstaple, Maidstone . . . mum and I followed him and we lived in all sorts of different houses and I went to all sorts of different schools. I never had enough time to make friends, so I lived in a world of my own. I preferred it that way. Dad always moved on because he got into trouble – he was too intransigent and always managed to put people's backs up.

`When we moved here and he got a job at Coombes, things began to be different. The manager at Coombes liked him, appreciated his skill and knowledge, and gave him promotion to a good job in quality control. It's changed dad's life, and now that mum's got a job at the Foodmart, things are better than they've ever been – better than any of us could have hoped for. Dad enjoys his work, which is a first.

`I didn't bother to enrol in school when we came here. There was no point. I've got my GCSE's, and didn't feel inclined to go any further with my studies – my grades weren't that good, anyway. I'd spent too long feeling out of place in too many new schools to want to spend any time actually doing schoolwork.

`I guess my parents felt guilty about the on-off nature of my childhood stability. At school I went to one or two counsellors because I had truancy trouble. They wanted me to blame it all on my parents – which I did, because that was what they wanted to hear – but actually, I don't blame my parents, particularly. Dad's just as alienated as I am. The only reason he's happy in his current job is because he hardly ever has to talk to anyone. He loves my mother, and me I suppose, but has never been able to properly handle his anger at never really belonging anywhere.

`I only met Eddy by chance a few months back, down by Larkshill playground. He came over and asked to take a few photos of me. I knew straight away what he was thinking of, but I was bored, broke and pissed off with life. He gave me money and clothes, and made me feel wanted. That's the thing. I was wanted; and he didn't lay a finger on me. He's into Asians and Hispanics, so I was okay.

`When I started doing massage, these guys would come. Sometimes they were unhappy, and they were so grateful for what I offered them – and it wasn't much, believe me – that it was like, for the first time ever, I was doing something useful. I was doing something that had some kind of meaning, even if it could be demeaning at times, and even dangerous, which is why Eddy was always around. I'm not the only one who works from that flat. There's another guy, who's a bit older than me – a Spaniard that lives there with Eddy.

`I guess that's pretty difficult to understand. Even I find it difficult to understand. But it made me start to feel things again, and it was only then, when I started to come to life, that I realised how I had been stuck for so long in my fantasy world of nothingness.

`Then I met Mel, and she really worked hard at getting to know me – you know, hanging around, coming out with all this small-talk shit. But it was all worth it, because through her I met you. But she kept on and on at me, until it came out that I was sleeping with you. And then it suddenly stopped, thank Christ. She couldn't even look at me after that, which was a relief. Then, a couple of weeks

155

ago, she invited herself round to my place. Seeing as she knew about us, I didn't see the harm in it. But maybe she had heard a rumour, or was just plain nosey, because she poked about whilst I was out of the room. After she'd left, I realised that my collection of porno pictures had been stolen.'

`So that's where Becky got them.'

Ian shrugged.

`Whatever.'

`What about this other guy that you work with?'

`Julio? He's great. I think that's why the whole thing works so well. We all like each other.'

He looked across at me and smiled, a thin, diffident smile.

`That's it, too,' he said. `Julio taught me a little bit about what it is to have a friend. Without him, I don't think I would have been able to have a friendship with you, or even be able to start to love you. He's the one who opened the door. And I didn't sleep with him, either. Sex is such a complication as far as I can see.'

He said this with a certain emphasis that made me wary.

`Why is it such a complication?' I asked. `Do you want to stop having sex with me, or something?'

`No,' he said slowly, `but I want to want to make love with you, not just go through the motions. I love you, Paul, I fancy you too because you're beautiful, but . . . '

`But what?'

`I need time.'

Now it was my turn to shrug. `If only I knew exactly what that meant.'

`You're right,' he said. `Maybe this thing between us can never work.'

I went back home that night feeling more confused than ever.

✳ ✳ ✳ ✳ ✳

The next morning, I knew there was something wrong. Duncan was even quieter than usual at breakfast. I'd only had three or four hours sleep and I couldn't hide the fact that I was tired.

`What time did you get in?' mum asked me.

`I don't know,' I said.

`Three-forty-five,' she said. `And you came in a taxi. Who paid for that, I'd like to know?'

I put some toast in the toaster and poured myself some tea. I didn't reply.

`Duncan and I have been talking,' she said. `We've decided you shouldn't see Adeline any more.'

`She's behind all this,' said Duncan.

I sat down slowly at the table. Addy? I'd thought they were going to confront me about Ian.

`You can't do this,' I said. `You can't make me stop seeing Addy. I've seen her every week for . . . forever.'

`Putting ideas into your head!' sneered Duncan.

`What has she been writing to you?' I asked, abruptly remembering the larger-than-usual envelope that she'd left the day before.

`Never you mind,' said mum.

`Interfering cow,' Duncan muttered. `Telling *us* what we should and shouldn't be doing in our own house.'

`You're not seeing Adeline again,' said mum, `and no arguing. And you've to be in by ten o'clock if you go out.'

`And whoever you go out with can come to the door,' said Duncan, `so that we can see who it is.'

`It's your own fault, Paul,' mum told me. `If you hadn't got into such bad company it would never have come to this.'

FOUR

`Okay,' said the restaurant manager. `This is your room. Drop your bag here and I'll take you down to the kitchens.'

My room was narrow – part of a larger room that had been partitioned off. The floor-covering was a sliver of worn brown lino; there was a chest of drawers at one end and a double bunk bed along the wall. A tiny, dirty skylight in the sloping roof let in a meagre trickle of light. I dumped my bag on the floor and wondered who I would be sharing with. I noticed that the white chest of drawers was marked on top with cigarette burns, and I felt my heart sink.

In the kitchens I was introduced to the head chef, who nodded dismissively at me, and was then taken through to the lower kitchen, where I met Warren, a man of about forty-five, with whom I was left. He was shortish, with mid-length greasy hair, and a good-looking face that was going jowly – as though the flesh had started to give in to gravity.

The washing up area was so well used that the wood of the service hatch had been worn away at the edges. The stainless steel of the sinks and drainers had a particular sheen from constant use. The ceiling was nicotine brown, and long, greasy, dust-clogged cobwebs hung down around the extractor fan.

`Right,' Warren said, `this is where you'll be working. I'll expect you down here by five-thirty am prompt, to get the early breakfast trays organised. At seven the restaurant opens, so we have to do toast, melba toast, teas and coffees, and get cracking on the washing up that starts coming in. At nine you can have a half-hour break, for a cooked breakfast, before finishing off the washing up, clearing the dining room and setting tables for lunch. Then you're finished, at around eleven. Lunch time staff do morning coffee, lunch and afternoon teas and set the tables for dinner. You come back at six-thirty and we get ready for dinner. That's the quietest time, when the first diners are in. By seven-thirty you'll be rushed off your feet with washing up and coffees, and errands to the store rooms and so on. Then, when all the diners have finished, you clear the dining room and set the tables for breakfast. You'll be finished around midnight. Sometimes earlier. Sometimes, especially on a Saturday, it can be a lot later.

`Don't talk to the head waiter or any of the chefs unless you are spoken to. Some of the waiters are bastards – you'll get a hang of that after a time – and most of the waitresses are okay. If you do your job well and conscientiously, you'll get a lot out of it.'

He turned away from me to wipe a surface. I seemed to have been instantly forgotten, but after a few moments he turned back to me.

`Oh, and by the way, we're sharing a room so you'd better not fucking snore like the boy before you.'

I went back up to my room and wondered how I was going to survive. When I'd been told that it was going to be a six day, sixty hour week I had had no clear idea of what that meant. Now, I felt overwhelmed by the prospect of such hard work.

I remembered phoning for the job and taking an afternoon off school to go for the interview. I'd been accepted on the spot by a congenial-looking hotel manager who had said kind things about my prospects once I'd learned the ropes.

`A large hotel like this,' he'd said, `has endless possibilities for a bright boy who works hard.'

Within three days of Ian saying he thought there might not be any future for us, and mum and Duncan forbidding me to see Addy, I'd secured the job and told them I was leaving.

`What about school?' mum had asked.

`Stuff school,' I'd said. `You both want me out of the house. You should be happy that I'm obliging.'

Duncan and mum had looked at each other then, and it made me feel hard and vulnerable at the same time when they didn't try to contradict me. I'd told them I would have to come back for my things once I'd found somewhere to

159

live outside the hotel, and then Duncan had driven me the four miles to the mainline station.

`About time,' he told me, by way of farewell.

I hadn't even seen Ian before I'd left. I was too confused about my feelings to know how to tell him, or even to know if I wanted to see him again. Perhaps he was right when he questioned whether our relationship could work.

I stood in that tiny room and busied myself unpacking my stuff into the bottom two drawers of the chest, then, stunned at myself for leaping into this new situation, I went for a walk, ending up in a busy MacDonalds, where I whiled away an hour or so. Later, back at the hotel, I read for a while on the upper bunk and ended up going to bed before ten.

Warren came in, half drunk, at half-past midnight. He swore, bashed about, threw his clothes indiscriminately around the room and then, once in bed, proceeded to snore excruciatingly.

I suppose I must have slept a little, because when the alarm went off I could hardly wake up enough to switch it off.

`Turn that fucking thing off!' Warren yelled, and punched the bottom of my bunk.

The alarm was by my pillow and I grappled with it for a few seconds before I could silence it.

`Shit,' Warren muttered, `it's only ten-past.'

He leaned out of bed and looked up at me.

`Don't do that,' he grumbled. `I've got an alarm that goes off at twenty-five-past. I'll get you up.'

It turned out that he kept his toothbrush in the lower kitchen – a useful habit. I followed him downstairs in the dark and, for the first hour, washed up and made toast in a dream. By nine o'clock I was so famished that I had stomach pains. At least the breakfast was good – and huge – when it came. But when I sat down to eat in the staff canteen, Warren went to sit with a junior cook and made it clear that I was not meant to join him. The junior cook was good-looking, but there was no way he'd be interested in me – I had lank hair already from the steam and the heat. It

160

didn't stop me looking, though, but he noticed after a while and sneered at me.

By the time I had helped to lay the tables for lunch it was ten-past-eleven and I was so shattered that I went upstairs and slept right through until three.

The evening was the same as the morning – plates, bowls, cutlery and glasses coming so fast that I couldn't keep up with them, and they began to build up higher and higher on the service hatch. I pulled them out, sorted and stacked them in the washing up machine as fast as I could, but it wasn't fast enough. And when the plates came out of the washer they were so hot that I could hardly bear to pick them up. And the waste – all that food I scraped into the bin, food that I would never have got to *see* at home, let alone eat . . .

'Don't worry,' one of the waitresses said to me at one point, 'it always gets like this in the middle of the evening.'

It was the first time anyone had spoken to me, except for Warren giving me orders. I tried to smile, but I was too hot from the steam and the rush.

As the glasses came in, Warren would pour the dregs of white wine into one jug and red into another. Taking ice from the main kitchen, he would pour a glass of iced white wine for himself every now and again, as soon as there was enough.

'Here,' he said begrudgingly when several half-full glasses came in at once, 'have some yourself.'

I did, but I was so hot that the wine went to my head and made me feel woozy. Later, when the rush had died down, Warren drank the red.

By midnight I could hardly stand up, as I laid the last covers for breakfast, and when I went to bed I wasn't bothered whether Warren was going to snore or not. Nobody had spoken to me all evening, except for that waitress, once, and Warren – who, I was now beginning to realise, regarded me as being too junior to be worthy of his attention.

I didn't even hear Warren's alarm the next morning. The first I knew was when he shook me hard.

161

'For fuck's sake,' he shouted, 'get up!'

I could hardly move. My back, arms and legs hurt. I staggered downstairs and made a start on coffees. When I put my hands in hot water for the first time, I cried out with pain, they were so raw.

'Christ,' he said, 'that's all I need – a faggot kitchen junior. Go and get some rubber gloves from the main kitchen.'

When I came back, he looked at me carefully.

'You are a faggot, aren't you?'

I didn't answer.

'Oh, great!' he muttered and went back to his work.

I couldn't believe that any human being could be asked to work so hard, for so long and for so little money. The morning stretched out in front of me like an endless nightmare, and by the time I finished I was too tired to even go and sleep. I just went up to my room and lay on my bunk and looked up at the ceiling.

By the fourth day I was beginning to get the hang of it, but it was still mindless hard work that left no time for anything other than food and rest. Thankfully, I didn't even have time to miss or think about Ian. I just got up, worked, rested, worked, ate and slept.

On the fifth day I had my accident. A wine glass had been put into a beer glass, where it had stuck. The bowl of the glass had broken off so that there was only a sharp stem sticking up, invisible at a cursory glance. It was the busiest part of the evening and I was cleaning glasses by hand whilst Warren stacked dishes into the washer. Holding the scourer, I put my gloved hand into the beer glass with a twisting motion and skewered myself neatly onto the broken stem.

I cried out in pain and dropped the glass, which bounced off the lino without breaking. I ripped off the glove and tried to see how bad the cut was, but blood was pouring from the wound and was already dripping onto the floor.

'Oh, shit,' Warren cursed when he saw the blood. 'Get Dave,' he called to one of the waitresses. Dave was the

162

restaurant manager and, when he came through, he looked at me as though I had cut myself deliberately in order to inconvenience him. The plates were piling higher and higher on the service hatch, and he glanced at my hand and said, `I haven't got time for this,' and left.

Warren grabbed my hand and held it under the cold tap, causing a stab of pain so sharp that I involuntarily pulled away. He tugged my hand back and thrust it into the stream of water again. People called for us to get them pots of coffee, more clean plates and cutlery. Everyone was getting more and more fraught, and Warren leaned over me and hissed in my ear, `Fucking fairy faggot. Trust you to cock everything up.'

The blood kept on coming, even after an ineffectual plaster had been applied. But it was slowing down, and so I put on a new pair of gloves and carried on washing the glasses, the fingers of my right hand slippery inside the glove with the oily smoothness of blood.

When it came to laying the tables for breakfast, there was an insistent throbbing pain in my hand. I'd put a new plaster on the cut, but it had soaked through again. When I was finished, I went and sat in the staff room and timidly peeled the plaster off. My hand had swollen alarmingly round the cut, which looked narrow and deep. I could just see, as I looked carefully, the top of a shard of glass. With my fingernails, I managed to grasp it and pull the sliver – which must have been over a centimetre long – from my hand. The blood started to flow again, but the relief of being rid of the splinter was wonderful. I sat and let the cut bleed for a while onto a paper napkin, then went to get another plaster.

Warren came out of the lower kitchen and glanced at me. I held up my splinter for him to see.

`You've got to put up with it,' he said, not unkindly. `You have to take it in your stride.'

*****

The following day I was awake before five-thirty. I felt a

kind of dread at the prospect of the day ahead. My hand had been throbbing in the night, and when I got up, I found that it had swelled up even further.

That morning was the worst morning of my life. I was in pain, I could hardly fit my rubber glove on, and it was difficult to move the fingers of my right hand. My duties were the same as ever, but although I knew what to do, they seemed insurmountable. Warren yelled at me several times to get a move on.

At eleven, I went upstairs and sat on my bed for some time, fighting a feeling of desolation so strong that if I gave in to it, I thought, I would never emerge from it. At twelve, I went to the chest of drawers and carefully packed my bag, then I crept down the back staircase and, once in the lobby, tried to walk out of the hotel as nonchalantly as possible.

`Hoi!' the receptionist called to me.

I didn't turn, but picked up my pace and ran from the revolving doors, my bag thumping rhythmically against my leg. No one followed me. I slowed down to a walk as soon as I was out of sight of the hotel and managed a smile when I thought of Warren having to do without me that evening.

Fuck them, I thought, *fuck them all.*

FIVE

We got a lift, in an old Ford Escort, from the funeral to the wake. The driver, a thin man called Mitch, who'd sat right up at the front in church, commiserated with Addy.

'Don't blame yourself,' he told her. 'It could never have been any different. You had to do it, Addy. It wasn't your fault.'

'How old was Jack when he died,' I asked.

'Forty-six,' Mitch said.

That sounded pretty old to me. Still, Adeline was thirty-six and she still looked stunning. I looked over at her and she reached out and grasped my hand, squeezing it so tight that it sent a stabbing pain through my fingers, making the knuckles throb where my cut had yet to fully heal. I didn't cry out, like I normally would. I left my hand there, being crushed, as Adeline tried to hold back her tears.

At the wake there were piles of food. I ate a dozen crab-sticks one after the other. I offered some to Addy. She wolfed two down and then nibbled a third carefully.

'I have to look after my figure,' she said, running her palms over svelte hips.

People kept on coming up and hugging Addy as though Old Jack had been really important to her. She smiled and sniffed and, after a while, she told them who I was.

And then everything changed.

'So you're Laura's boy, then, tch, tch,' they said. 'It must have been tough,' they said. 'But at least Addy's been there for you.' And they looked at me as though the past had spat right in their faces.

'What is all this?' I asked Addy. 'Why am I the centre of attention all of a sudden?'

'Are you? Mmm, I suppose you are.'

I ate a few more crab-sticks. I think I get a buzz out of the chemicals. Then a woman right beside me mentioned Old Jack's final lover – the one he had when he died – and I saw him being pointed out. It was Mitch. I remembered him sitting in the front pew, rigid, staring straight ahead all the time. Life is weird. He'd been so attentive to Adeline in the car, but he was the one who'd *lost the most.*

`Ten years they were together,' this person said, `or would have been next month.'

`Hold on,' I said. `This guy Jack, was he . . . ?'

The man smiled at me.

`Gay? Of course he was. Didn't Laura tell you? No, I suppose she wouldn't. Well, he was as queer as they come. Used to boast that he'd never laid a finger on a woman in his life.'

That did it for me. I felt strangled by my trust in Adeline. I'd always believed her – always. I'd never questioned her, never asked myself if what she was telling me was true. Her words had always been too sincere for that, too real, too important. I'd never doubted her when she'd said it was important to let love be love, whoever it was I fancied. I'd never doubted her when she'd said to put up with mum and Duncan because things would be alright in the end. I hadn't doubted her, despite my misgivings, when she'd told me that Ian loved me, or when she said she would always be there for me no matter what a stupid mess I made of my life.

`What's the matter?' she asked when she saw my face.

`You lied,' I said, astonished. `You lied to me, Adeline. Why did you do that? You told me you would never, ever lie to me. But you said that you and Old Jack Butler were lovers, and that was a lie.'

✳ ✳ ✳ ✳ ✳

I took the train back home, but instead of getting off at the usual stop, I got off at the one before and took a bus to Addy's place. It was after five when I got there, but she wasn't home from work yet. I let myself in, dropped my bag in the hall, and made myself some coffee. I had spent my last pound on the bus fare – I had run away before being paid at the hotel.

Addy came home just before six.

`Paul, at last!' she exclaimed, `but your hand? What happened?'

I let her take a look at it as I explained about the hotel, and Warren, and my room.

'Come through,' she said. 'Let me bathe it properly, it looks terrible.'

As my hand was soaking, she sighed.

'I was so worried. Ian's been over several times, looking for you. I phoned Laura and Duncan but they wouldn't say anything – only that you'd left. Ian's been in a real state. You should have talked to him before you left. You're not going back to this hotel are you?'

'No. I've missed less than a week of school. I reckon I'll be able to catch up.'

'What a stupid idea, to leave and go off like that. You should have talked to me if you couldn't stand being at home any more.'

'I just wanted to get away for a while, that's all,' I said.

Once my hand was bathed and bandaged, I borrowed some money from Addy again.

'Tell Ian how things are. I'll work something out and maybe I can meet him here?'

'You can come here any time. How many times do I have to tell you?' Addy sighed. 'Ian's a wonderful young man. We had a long talk and we both opened up a lot. He badly missed you, you know.'

I had mixed feelings as I returned home – none of them comfortable. The house looked exactly the same, and why shouldn't it? I'd only been gone six days. I let myself into the hall, put my bag in the kitchen doorway and walked into the front room. Mum and Duncan were sitting watching tv. I didn't say a word, just walked into the room and sat down and began to watch too.

Mum looked startled and glanced over to Duncan to see how he would react. He glanced at me, then purposefully glared at the screen.

'I'm back,' I said at last.

There was a long pause whilst none of us spoke. The tv droned on for some time before mum spoke.

'What happened?' she asked.

'It was terrible,' I said. 'I packed it in.'

Duncan tried to ignore me, but I could sense the mounting tension and eventually he had to speak.

167

`Oh, great,' he said, `you packed it in? So is that what you're going to do all your life – run away from things as soon as they get hard? You're that afraid of real work in a man's world, huh? And you think that if someone ever makes you do some work, that you can come crawling back to us? Well, you can't. You're not welcome here any more. The day you left for that hotel was the best day I've had in this house. What makes you think we want you back?'

`Duncan,' mum said, `it's only for another couple of months.'

`I don't give a toss how long it is. He's not welcome here.'

`I'll go and put my bag up in my room,' I said. `Then I'm going out.'

I went upstairs. My room was exactly as it had been, except that I noticed, immediately, that the buff envelope was gone. I sat on the bed and heard Duncan's footsteps on the stairs.

`Don't think you can come back here and find that things haven't changed,' he shouted. `Don't think you can go out whenever you like until however late you like. If you're staying here, you're staying here to work. You are not going to go out. You are not bringing friends here. You can go to school, come back from school, and you can work. Got it?'

I stared at him, at his tensed eyes and clenched fists and I nodded.

`Paul,' mum called, `have you eaten? There's some kedgeree in the fridge. I'll put some in the microwave if you like.'

`Thanks mum,' I called and stood up. I sidled past Duncan and as I started down the stairs, I turned to him.

`Thanks for the warm welcome home,' I said.

Duncan leapt at me when I said this. He caught me half way down the stairs and, grabbing my shoulders, shoved me hard against the wall.

`Watch out, you!' he choked, thrusting his face so close to mine that I could feel the spittle on my cheek as he

168

hissed. `Anyone else would have thrown you out – or have gone to the police. You should feel lucky that we're giving you any chance at all.'

`Duncan!' mum shouted. `Leave him alone.'

Duncan cuffed me across the head and, leaving me leaning against the wall, went down to get himself another beer from the fridge.

`You always do that, don't you?' mum said to me as I walked into the kitchen. `You always make him angry. Why don't you just do as you're told sometimes?'

`I see,' I said, `it's my fault that he hits me.'

`Yes,' she said, `it is. If only you weren't so defiant.'

I couldn't bring myself to answer her, so I sat and started on the kedgeree.

`That Ian,' she whispered. `I found those pictures, you know, in your room. They're disgusting. Delinquent. I burnt them before Duncan could see them, thank God, or he'd have *murdered* you. What are you doing with your life, Paul? I don't understand you at all. Not at all.'

* * * * *

The next day at school I had some explaining to do, but I'm one of the brightest pupils and my home life is a bit of an open book, so – in spite of mum's previous assurance that I'd left for good – I got away with my sudden absence and equally sudden return. Mel was openly gleeful when she saw me, as if, by my sorry predicament, I had come to represent some great triumph for her. Pug shrugged when I said hello and turned away.

I sat and tried to concentrate on my lessons, but I was preoccupied with how I was going to get to see Ian again. How could I find an excuse to get out of the house long enough to meet him? It occurred to me to skip school to see him during the day, but I found that, even in so short a time, I had a lot of catching up to do . . . I borrowed a whole pile of notes from the previous week and set off home to make some sense of them.

When I got back, mum was already there.

169

`Hi,' I said. `Are you okay?'

`He's gone,' she said, slowly, turning her bloodshot eyes to me. She had a livid bruise on her cheek. `He walked out.'

`Duncan?'

`Yes.'

`Why?'

`We had a row. About you. About Addy, too. He found something out about her that made him go wild. God, Paul, I've seen him go berserk with you, but he's never been like that with me. Never!'

`When did this happen?'

`After you left for school this morning.'

`But he's not even due back from work yet? How do you know he's gone?'

`I know Duncan,' she said, `and anyway, he's taken the overnight bag – you know, the black one with the tartan panels. And then he always comes home for lunch. But he didn't today. He's gone.'

`Weren't you at work at lunch time?' I asked.

`I couldn't face it,' she replied. `I phoned in sick.'

`Oh, mum,' I went over and put my arms round her, but she shrugged me off.

`Don't *oh, mum* me,' she said, `it was you who caused all this. If you hadn't come home this would never have happened. It's your fault this happened, Paul, it's your fault.'

She dropped her head and began to cry. I stood and watched and felt helpless.

`Look,' I said, `you need to be on your own.'

`Yes,' she sniffed, `go out if you like. It would be better for you not to be here if Duncan does comes back.'

`I won't be late.'

She didn't answer. I went upstairs and changed into an old pair of jeans and then left for Addy's place.

✳ ✳ ✳ ✳ ✳

`What did you do that would make Duncan go off his trolley?' I asked Addy as I lay lengthwise on her sofa.

170

`Really, it wasn't anything so terrible,' she said. `Let's not talk about it.'

`Please, Addy,' I said, `tell me the truth.'

`Truth?' she asked.

`I want something I can understand, that's all,' I told her. `I want something I can believe in.'

`Belief?' she said. `Look, Paul, appearances are deceptive. Don't start looking for anything too definitive. I mean, you believed a certain thing about Ian, didn't you? And then you were given those pictures, which made you believe something else. Actually, neither of the things that you believe about Ian are the truth. The truth is far too complicated for us to ever see it properly.'

`What are you trying to say to me?' I asked. `And what *did* you do?'

`I can't tell you now. But what I will say is that in this world you always have to keep an open mind.'

Ian phoned later on, and we talked for a while. We arranged to meet at Addy's the following evening – Saturday.

`I'll talk to you properly then,' he said. `I want to say what I have to say when you're in my arms.'

✽✽✽✽✽

The next morning I got up and went downstairs. Mum was still in bed. There was no sign of Duncan. I made breakfast and took some up to her. She was lying, wide awake, looking out of the window.

`I can't face it, Paul, I just can't face it,' she said. `All those shelves. Please, do you mind, could you phone Mr Marston and tell him I'm still not well.'

SIX

`I didn't lie to you about Old Jack,' Addy said to me. `I DID live with him. We WERE lovers.'

`But Old Jack Butler was gay!' I cried. `He couldn't have loved you. At least, not like you said.'

`He did,' Adeline assured me.

`How can I believe that?' I asked, more confused than ever. `Ask him over there. Ask Mitch. Old Jack Butler only loved men.'

Addy smiled then, a strange, frightening smile that seemed to come from a long way off. It appeared on her face like wind blooming over still water, but it didn't cover the wariness in her eyes.

`Oh, but you see,' she said slowly, `I was a man. Once.'

I wasn't ready to hear this. I suddenly felt weightless. Mitch glanced over and smiled sadly at us.

`Today,' she said, `is to be the end of secrets between us. I needed a reason to tell you this. What better occasion than Old Jack's funeral? I should perhaps have told you before, but I have an agreement, in writing, with your mother not to tell you until your eighteenth birthday.'

`That's only six weeks away.'

`Quite. And anyway, under certain circumstances I would have told you, in spite of my agreement. But eighteen has a certain feel to it that seems right for explanations, though in the end, perhaps, the time is never right until you are tripped up by the facts. Maybe I was just waiting for this to happen. Maybe that's why, deep down, I brought you here today.'

`So that you could tell me that you used to be a man?'

`Yes.'

`You waited for someone's funeral to tell me this?'

`Not just anyone's funeral, Paul.'

`No. This guy Jack was your lover. Okay. I see that now; but it's kind of difficult to take it in.'

I grabbed a glass of wine from the table next to me and took a gulp.

`That's why you were so acceptant of me being gay,' I said,

172

`because you'd had a gay relationship yourself.'

`Partly,' she said, `and, also, partly because I can be a pretty sensible person at times.'

`So how come you got involved with Laura and me and all that stuff?'

`Well, that's it, you see,' Addy breathed, `the fact is – I'm your dad.'

`Oh,' I said, and suddenly I was too surprised to disbelieve her. `Oh . . . '

`Yes,' she said, `I'm your dad. But I was like this inside – like I am now. That's why I had to leave Jack, even though we loved each other. I had to have my operation. I had to have it, even if it meant giving up on love, or at least love with Jack; even if it meant I had to live a half-anonymous life and keep clear of your gossipy neighbourhood. There was no other way I could ever be myself. And that's why Laura hated me – because I left her for a man . . . Because I became a woman.'

Adeline looked at me. What do you do when your best woman-friend turns out to be your father? But Addy was so many things to me – had always been a parent to me in all but name.

`That's why you come to see me every Saturday,' I realised.

`Parental duty, do you mind?'

`That you come to see me, or that you never told me who you were?'

`Both.'

How could I mind? After all those years, all that reassurance. How could I forget her shoulder so often used for tears; the vulnerability that she never hid; the way she always shared my fears? How could I doubt her, or reject her? She stood there, eyes sparkling from a cocktail of emotion, arms half extended, waiting for me to say something.

I took the crumpled Kleenex from her sleeve and dabbed her eyes.

`You've smudged your make-up,' I said. `I don't want you to look anything but your best. After all, you are the most exquisitely beautiful woman here.'

She took me in her arms, then, and tucked my head against her breast and cried into my hair.

`Paul,' she whispered, `oh, Paul.'

173

I broke from her embrace.

`The letters!' I exclaimed. `The letters you left on the kitchen table for mum.'

`Money,' she said, `for your upkeep. You think I'd write letters to Laura for pleasure?'

`All this time,' I said, stunned, `you've been paying. All this time, and you never told me.'

She shrugged.

`It was worth it.'

`Come on,' I said. `Let's go back to your place. I want you to tell me everything.'

`Okay. But there are a few people I must say goodbye to.'

❊ ❊ ❊ ❊ ❊

`I was seventeen when I started going out with Laura,' she said. `A little younger than you are now. It was just a lark. I didn't really know what I wanted in life, so I drifted into an affair with her. Everyone else was having sex, or at least pretending that they were having sex, and so I decided to find out what it was all about.

`My name was Derek – Del,' she laughed. `It seems so strange to say that name now. Derek. Del. I was quite good-looking, too, for a boy.'

She got up and stood in front of the mirror.

`But I knew,' she said, `I knew inside that I should look like this.'

She turned to me and smiled.

`Laura and I hardly even knew each other. We were two kids who fucked a few times because of peer pressure. If you hadn't come along we would have happily parted and never spoken again. As it was, I agreed to live with her and set up home. We didn't marry, because even then I knew I wouldn't be able to pass the happy-young-husband test. We lived two streets down from where you are now, in a tiny terraced house that has now been demolished. I loved you and had nothing in common with Laura. As time passed I couldn't even bring myself to touch her, let alone make love to her. It wasn't her fault, but it made us both miserable.

`I fancied boys,' she said, `but when I was first introduced
to the gay scene, it didn't feel right. There were all these men
who enjoyed being men fancying men. I wanted to be a
woman fancying men. I slept with a few guys, without
Laura knowing, but it wasn't anything serious and wouldn't
have led to anything if I hadn't met Jack. He liked me as I
was – slender and boyish. He loved me so much, it made me
realise what I was sacrificing for the sake of a child. My life
for yours, in fact. That's how I saw it and, truthfully, that's
how it was. So I moved in with Jack on my nineteenth
birthday, and we were happy for a time. But I wanted to
wear dresses and look like a woman. He wanted me to look
like a boy. We talked through the whole cross-dressing thing
and we decided that I was transsexual rather than
transvestite. It was hard for him to let me seek treatment,
but he loved me and knew I had to do it.

`There was quite a lot going on in terms of gender re-
assignment at that time, and so I got all the details and
started on my course of hormonal treatment. As you can see,
I have quite large hips and small hands. I was a pretty
convincing woman right from the start, unlike some of the
other transsexuals that I knew who had a hell of a trouble
with adam's apples and bandy legs and skinny bums – all
sorts. I was lucky.

`I had to live as a woman full-time, and Jack – well, Jack
as you've already said, loved men. After a time, especially
after my breasts began to develop, it was the same for us as
it had been with me and Laura – he couldn't bring himself to
touch me. He used to look at my dick and say what a
terrible waste to lose such a beautiful appendage. It was an
unhappy time for us both, and eventually I left to live in a
bed-sit on my own.

`My new identity wasn't easy. People are incredibly
judgmental, as you know. It would have been easier to move
to another town where no one knew me, but I wanted to be
near you – and so I made do with living here and working
elsewhere. I took this flat in Lawley Wood and didn't show
my face round your way, except, much later, to pick you up
on Saturdays. Luckily, Laura kept quiet about my new

identity. As far as I know, she told her friends that I ran off to America. I lost almost all my own friends; I had to change jobs – I had to *find* a job where being transsexual didn't matter, which wasn't easy, I can tell you. I finally managed to get work in an ad agency that was run by two gay men. It's a twenty mile drive each way, but that suited me. So, I guess it's worked out okay, finally. I saw you every Saturday. Laura hated that, but she needed the money and, besides, I could have fought for access in the courts if necessary. She never told Duncan who I really was, until now. I guess she thought – rightly as it appears – that he wouldn't take it well.

`I just kept in the background and watched you grow up and loved you as best I could. When I realised you were gay, I was pleased. If only I'd been gay, then I wouldn't have had all the physical trauma of my sex reassignment. But there we are. There are problems either way, aren't there? I always felt guilty that you didn't have a happy homelife. But what could I do except give you as much support as I knew how?'

The doorbell rang as she said this. She didn't move, but looked across at me and smiled.

`For you, I think.'

I went to the door. It was Ian, looking smart, wearing dark, well-cut trousers and a black cotton shirt.

`Hi,' he said and hugged me hard. `Don't do that again, please,' he whispered. `Don't go away without a word and leave me.'

`I won't,' I whispered back.

`To be a washer-upper too, according to Addy,' he said. `Really!'

He pulled me closer and drew his lips close to my ear.

`I've given it up,' he murmured, `the day you left, I phoned Eddy. I haven't been since – and I don't miss it.'

He turned and took my elbow, pulling me gently into the room.

`Hello Addy,' he said, and kissed her. `Have you told him?'

`Yes,' she sighed.

`And?'

`And he still loves me. We are still friends.'

Ian sat beside me.

`I wish I had a father like Addy,' he said, and we all laughed because it sounded so strange.

`Why did you do it?' he asked. `Why did you run away from me?'

`From you?' I said. `Is that what you think?'

`Of course. If you were running away from home, you would have come to Addy.'

`It didn't feel like I was running from you,' I said. `I just needed to get away so that I could think.'

`But you came back.'

`Yes.'

`And did you think?'

`No. I had neither the time, the energy, nor the inclination.'

He smiled at me, the most tender smile I had yet seen.

`But how about you, Ian?' Addy asked. `How are things with you?'

Ian turned to me.

`Your mother's a cow, do you know that?' he said to me. `She told my mother about those photo sessions I did. She went up to her at the check-outs and accused her of letting me corrupt you. Right there, in front of everyone. As if I could have done a thing like that . . . '

`No wonder she didn't want to go in to work,' I said. `What did your mother do?'

`Not much herself, but she told my father. _He_ wanted to kill me. Fortunately he's not like Duncan – though verbal violence is bad enough.'

He looked at me and took my hand.

`It's funny,' he said, `I always thought I was the strong one – doing all that massage stuff; getting into new situations and meeting new people, whilst you did schoolwork at home. But it turns out that, actually, I was the weak one. I was the one who moped about in the house all day. And I didn't meet new people, either. I interacted with their bodies, that's all, not their minds. You got up and did something when things got too bad – you had the strength to walk away.

`I stood there, at home, my father yelling at me, and I thought: *what the fuck am I doing here*? It was crazy, so I took my strength from you. I stood and he yelled and I went calmer and calmer inside and I told him, very quietly, that I knew when I wasn't welcome and that he'd be happy to discover that I was planning to move out as soon I could find somewhere to go.'

`God, Ian,' I said, `where can you go?'

`That,' said Addy, `isn't a problem. This flat isn't exactly huge, but it'll be fine for a while. We can set up the mattress here, behind the settee, and it'll hardly show. I've been through it all with Ian. He came over yesterday and we talked it through.'

`Brilliant!' I said. `I'll be able to come over and see you both whenever I want.'

`No,' Ian smiled, `you've missed the point. I'm not expecting to sleep on the mattress alone.'

I paused.

`What, you mean me? You mean I should move in here too?'

`How much stuff have you got?' he asked.

`Not much really, or at least not much that I'd want to keep. There's my schoolwork of course . . . '

`Paul,' said Addy, `it's not perfect, I know, but it's not much further into school from here than from your place. There's a desk in my bedroom that you can work at. I know we'll probably be at each other's throats, living so close in such a small place, but we love each other and that's going to count for a hell of a lot.'

`And your exams will be over in a few weeks.'

`All that work, though!' I said. `All that revision.'

`All that time together,' said Ian.

`And no violence,' said Addy, `no atmospheres.'

`Okay,' I said, `okay. But what'll I do about mum?'

`She'll agree,' said Addy. `Don't worry about that.'

`But she'll be on her own.'

`No,' Addy smiled, `as soon as you leave home, Duncan will creep back to her. That's the kind of man he is. You think he's strong? He's the weakest man I've ever met.'

178

Also Available

Packing It In
David Rees

This collection of essays, written and arranged to form a
year long diary, opens with an all too brief visit to Australia,
continues with a tour of New Zealand and a final visit to a
much loved San Francisco, before returning to familiar
Europe (Barcelona, Belgium Rome) and new perspectives on
the recently liberated Eastern Bloc countries (highly
individual observations of Moscow, St Petersburg, Odessa
and Kiev). Written from the distinctive and idiosyncratic
point of view of a singular gay man, this is a book filled with
acute and sometimes acerbic views, written with a style that
is at once easily conversational and utterly compelling.

*'Rees achieves what should be the first aim of any travel writer, to
make you regret you haven't seen what he has seen . . .'*

Gay Times

ISBN 1-873741-07-3
£6.99

Vale of Tears: A problem shared
Peter Burton & Richard Smith

Culled from ten years of *Gay Times's* popular Vale of Tears problem page, this book, arranged problem-by-problem in an alphabetical sequence, is written in question and answer format and covers a wide range of subjects.

Problems with a lover? Who does the dishes? Interested in infantilism? Why is his sex drive lower than yours? Aids fears? Meeting the family? How to survive Christmas? Suffering from body odours? Piles? Crabs? Penis too small? Foreskin too tight? Trying to get rid of a lover?

Vale of Tears has some of the answers – and many more. Although highly entertaining and sometimes downright humorous, this compilation is very much a practical handbook which should find a place on the shelves of all gay men.

'An indispensable guide to life's problems big or small . . .'
Capital Gay

ISBN 1-873741-05-7
£6.99